BELOVED BY YOU

MOLLY SLOAN

© Copyright 2018 - All rights reserved.

It is not legal to reproduce, duplicate, or transmit H of this document in either electronic means or in printed format. Recording of this publication is strictly prohibited and any storage of this document is not allowed unless with written permission from the publisher except for the use of brief quotations in a book review.

This book is a work of fiction. Any resemblance to persons, living or dead, or places, events or locations is purely coincidental.

DEDICATION

To my sweet RSL. Who encourages me everyday to be the change I want to see in the world.

ACKNOWLEDGMENT

To D.A.- You are my champion!

CHAPTER ONE: TOUCHDOWN

"Aren't you that model?"

Andrew Atherton pulled off his expensive Hi-Fi headphones and asked, "What did you say?"

The woman seated next to him on the plane repeated herself. "Aren't you that model? The one that used to be on those diamond ads? 'The Face of Atherton' or something?"

He always hated this question. Yes, Andrew had done some modeling for his family's diamond empire when he was in college. His sister Claudia used to tease him and call him The Adonis of Atherton because, evidently, she thought he was good-looking. But, since then, he'd gone on to get his MBA from The London School of Business, and now headed the

Acquisitions division of the family business. These days, the only thing Claudia teased him about was the fact that she was the CEO of the company and, technically, his boss.

But the fact was, they were both billionaires. Atherton Diamonds has been the leading diamond manufacturer in the world for more than two hundred years. And, Claudia and Andrew were the only heirs to the business.

Looking back at the woman seated next to him, Andrew realized that he really didn't want to talk. They had a long thirteen-hour flight ahead of them before landing in Botswana. Andrew just smiled at her and shook his head and said nicely, "I'm sure you must be mistaken." Placing the headphones back over his ears, Andrew reclined his plush First Class seat back to the sleeping position, closed his eyes and began to dream…

"I'm blinded by your hair! All I can see is red!" Andrew laughed as Janet straddled him. Her full breasts were tantalizingly close to his mouth. Her body was lightly dusted with freckles, and it turned him on to think of licking each freckle one a time. "Mmmmmm…come here, you vixen."

The dream fast-forwarded. They were in a pub in

London and Janet was angry with him about something. They were fighting.

"All the women keep hitting on you and you just sit there and smile. I think you like all the attention! That's why you became a model." Janet was both crying and angry — something Andrew never understood about women.

"I do not. I just think their come-on lines are funny. Really. Who says, 'Is it hot in here or is it just you?' Not even my roommate Cole says that." But Janet wasn't having it, and the next thing he knew, her red ponytail was swinging as she stormed out of the pub. "Come on, Red!"

The dream changed again. They were in bed in his flat. White sheets tangled around them as sweat ran down his back. Her legs were over his shoulders and they moved in unison. The only sounds were the moans of their lovemaking. Oh, how he loved making love with Janet.

His heart began to pound in his sleep as the dream became his nightmare. The day he came home to find the "Dear John" letter that she was leaving — going back to America. "Don't bother looking me up. I won't take your calls." Andrew had been devastated. Yes, they had problems. But couples should be able to work through them. How could he live the rest of his life without Janet?

"Ladies and Gentlemen, we are beginning our initial descent into Sir Seretse Khama International Airport. Please place your seat backs and tray tables…"

Andrew awoke with a start. What a terrible dream! Except that it had been real. Gazing out the window as the city lights of Gaborone, Botswana came into view, Andrew reflected on the dark period in his life after Janet broke up with him. "I wonder what ever happened to her?"

"Did you say something?" The woman seated next to him looked overly eager to think Andrew's comments might have been directed at her. Andrew just smiled and shook his head "no" again.

CHAPTER TWO: THE FORGOTTEN GOODBYE

Janet Girard hated hospitals. One would think that after spending so much time in them that she would have developed some sort of resistance to the feelings that the antiseptic smells, hushed voices, and stern faces in white coats stirred in her, but repeated exposure had only seemed to make her senses keener. The fine hairs on her body notice the shift of energy in the room. Noticed how the mouth of the last nurse that came in to check Gouta's vitals set in a grim line before she made a few notes in her chart and walked out. Noticed how, even as she cuddled her son in close to her side, Gouta struggled with each breath.

Her name meant gold in Setswana, and the day Janet met her, her dark skin had shone like a layer of gold was hidden just beneath the surface. With her bright smile and beaming optimism, no one would have even guessed that she was sick. And her little boy, Oba, wide-eyed and shy, who hid behind her leg when strangers spoke to him…that sweet face. It was almost inevitable that Janet would get attached. She tried so hard not to do that. There were so many kids at A Place of Grace that she couldn't afford to give a piece of herself away to every child in her keep. Practically every child in the orphanage was there because his or her parents had died of AIDS.

Botswana had once had the unfortunate privilege of having the second-highest human immunodeficiency virus infection rate in the world, with one in three adults infected. This meant that A Place of Grace was filled to capacity and demand for beds was growing by the month.

Things had definitely improved in the fifteen years since she started her humanitarian work in this part of the world. Safe sex practice was taught and was now the norm so fewer new cases were being diagnosed, which gave Janet some hope that there would be fewer boys like Oba. But that really didn't help Oba, did it? Janet shook her head to fight off the tears that threatened to flow.

Her dear friend Gouta was dying. Probably today.

And Oba—poor Oba. How does a five-year-old watch his mother die?

"Janet?" Gouta whispered, lifting her oxygen mask away from her face.

"Yes?" Janet stood and wiped her hands on her pant legs. Anxiety had clung to her all day. The end was so close that it felt like another presence in the room. And when she came to stand next to her friend's bed, she could tell that she knew it too.

"Our little king is sleepy, I think."

Janet looked at him and smiled. "I think you're right."

"I'm not tired," Oba said, but it was a half-hearted protest. His eyes drooped as he laid his head back down on the pillow that was propping his head up on the chair. "I am awake."

Janet walked around to the opposite side of the bed and picked up the five-year-old. He wrapped himself around her and nuzzled his head into the crook of her neck. Since Gouta had been sick, Janet spent more and more time with Oba. She was practically a second mother to him at this point.

"Hm. He is so long. Pretty soon he'll be too big to carry that way," Gouta said. Her smile was sad and her eyes went glassy with tears.

"We'll see you tomorrow, yeah?" Janet said,

reaching for Gouta's hand and giving it a gentle squeeze.

"Tomorrow," she said, but there was no promise in the word.

Janet shifted the weight of the dozing child in her arms and left the hospital room, ignoring the chill that had passed through her as Gouta's fingers slipped from hers.

It wasn't right. It wasn't fair. Just eight months ago, Gouta had been a beautiful young woman, brimming with potential, and now she was wasting away in a hospital bed from a disease that still had no cure, but was so easily prevented. How many more children have to face this before something is done to stop the crisis? It was absolutely heartbreaking to see.

"Are you hungry?" Janet asked as they crossed the street, Oba's tiny hand in hers. "We can stop and get you something if you're hungry."

"I'm not hungry," Oba said. His voice was solemn. It was almost as if the same wariness clung to him that had bothered Janet when she was sitting next to Gouta's bed in the hospital. He was such a sweet, sensitive boy. He knew what was happening.

"How about some ice cream? I could go for a

vanilla cone right now. What about you? Do you want to get—"

"I didn't kiss mama goodbye!" Oba's eyes grew wide in terror as he yanked Janet to a stop in the middle of the crowded sidewalk.

She stroked the back of his hand with her thumb. "It's all right," she said. "Just be sure to give her double the kisses tomorrow."

"No!" he said, snatching his hand free. "I want to go back and kiss mama goodbye!"

Janet squatted down to get at his eye level. "Oba, your mama was very tired and you're very tired. Let's just get back to the—"

"No! I want to kiss mama goodnight!" he shouted defiantly and before Janet could react, he squirmed out of her grasp and took off.

She always forgot how fast little kids were. Oba was small for his age. Janet had at least three feet on him and most of that was legs, but Oba evaded her grasp with frightening ease. With his little legs and arms pumping, he barrelled down the sidewalk, heading back the way they came, heading straight for the intersection.

"Oba!" she shrieked, shoving people out of the way now.

The light had changed and heavy traffic sped

through the intersection. Oba stepped off the curb and Janet dove for him. Their bodies collided and she pulled him into her chest and rolled onto her side at the same time, hoping to take the full blow of the fall. With his tiny body tucked against her, momentum rolled them into the intersection. Janet screwed her eyes closed and prayed to a god that she didn't believe in. Brakes screeched all around them and her back was pelted with gravel.

Janet was terrified to open her eyes but she was sure that she felt the heat of an engine block on her shoulder. She just held her breath and crushed the boy against her while chanting. "We're okay, we're okay," into his ear.

"Miss?" A voice called out. "Miss, are you all right?"

Was she all right? Janet did a quick assessment. Her toes wiggled. Her knees still worked. Her right arm felt like it was on fire but that was understandable considering that she had slid on it across rough blacktop, but otherwise, she felt fine.

"Oba?" she said, holding the boy away from her so that she could see his face. There was a gash on his forehead and his eyes looked a bit unfocused. "Oba? Oba, speak to me. Are you okay?"

"My head hurts," he said finally then began to cry.

"Miss, pass me the boy. Let's get the two of you out from under there."

Under?

It was then that Janet looked up and realized that heat she felt on her shoulder was from an engine, they were under a large truck.

"Oh, my god!" She passed Oba to the man and slowly, gingerly, scooted out from underneath the truck. Once she was out, she tried to stand up her head swam and she faltered.

"Whoa! Miss, are you okay? Oh my god. The boy came out of nowhere—"

"I know. He was upset… he ran away from me…" The world started to dim around the edges, but slowly like some was closing heavy theater curtains.

"Miss!"

She was passing out. It wasn't an unfamiliar feeling, but it was a frustrating one. "Oba…" she slurred reaching for the boy. She needed to tell someone where to take him. She had to tell someone who to call. "Call Place of…Place of…"

"I got ya'."

Strong arms scooped her up, cradling her against a broad chest. The voice was American and vaguely familiar. Janet looked up to see who had come to her rescue.

"Janet?" the deep, familiar voice with a thick New York accent said.

Her vision was blurry. She must have a head injury. She blinked once…then twice. The man's face slowly came into view.

She must have a severe concussion because this was the face of a man that she hadn't seen or spoken to in nearly a decade. Yes, she had a severe brain injury. There was a big gash in her head, it was gushing blood. Maybe some of her brains had leaked out on the pavement. That had to be it.

"Janet, it's me."

She frowned. "No…it can't be you."

"Yes, Janet. It's Andrew. Andrew Atherton."

"You've got to be fucking kidding me," Janet said, then promptly passed out.

CHAPTER THREE: DRIVEN

"Where have you been?" Andrew was completely stunned to see Janet standing in front of him. He had just been dreaming about her on the plane!

He'd seen the woman dart out in front of the lead car, with her pale skin and red hair flying out behind her like a flag, and for a second he wondered if he were still dreaming. Of all the trucks to dive in front of, she chose the lead one in his caravan as they made their way through Francistown, heading back to the hotel after spending the day exploring a potential mine site. Part of him was ready to call this divine timing, as if the man upstairs finally decided to answer the pleas he sent up years ago, by throwing her right into his path.

Andrew had spent a lot of money and wasted a lot of time trying to find her when she ran off, seven years ago. It took him four of those years to get over her and then another two to finally admit that he never really would be over her. So, he'd thrown himself into work and a few meaningless romances here and there. But now, here she was. Running out into traffic, sacrificing her life to save a little boy. *Typical Janet*, he thought.

Janet was looking a little woozy and so Andrew decided to wait on the questions until after she was checked out at the local hospital. "Actually, let's get you and the boy to the hospital. Come, get in my car."

Dazed, Janet and the boy hobbled into the back seat of the limo. Andrew was half-expecting her to refuse and to insist on walking. She was stubborn like that.

As the doors closed, the partition that separated the back seat from the front rolled down. "Should I cancel the dinner reservation or do you think we'll make it in time?" Fiona asked.

Fiona Durant was his Personal Assistant—and former lover, but that was insignificant now. She ran his personal and private life like a well-oiled machine and their brief interlude didn't affect her ability to do her job. It's not like they ever loved each other... it was just a relationship of convenience that ended when it became inconvenient.

"Go ahead and cancel, Fi. I'm staying here until I can see Janet and make sure that she's all right."

She raised an inquisitive brow and pivoted away from him as she brought her phone to her ear.

"You do realize that you've done your part, right? You don't have to hang around to wait and see if she's okay. You got her to the hospital. That was chivalrous enough."

"Nah, I'm staying."

Winston Konteh was the head of the African division of Atherton Diamonds and was still in the limo. After Janet and Oba got in, Winston leaned over to Andrew and whispered, "Do you know her?"

"Yeah, that's Janet," Andrew whispered back. Janet and Oba appeared to be dozing in their seats, so he continued in a low voice.

"Who?"

"Janet! You know—"

"The red-haired minx that ruined your life? That Janet?"

Andrew winced. "She didn't ruin my life exactly—"

"Those were your words, mate. Not mine."

He may have spent one too many nights deep in the bottle, trying to figure out where he had gone so wrong and how he would win her back.

"But what is she doing here anyway?"

"I don't know which is why I need to stay here until—"

"Well, I'm fine," said Janet who was most definitely not sleeping.

"Hey, Red," Andrew said sheepishly.

"Yeah. Not sleeping." She glared at him. "I have a cracking headache."

Damn. Even all scuffed up from the accident and pissed off at him, she was still gorgeous. Her auburn curls were wound into something that looked as if she would have a terrible time detangling. He'd always said she had Disney Princess hair and that hadn't changed. But the African sun had darkened her complexion from its usual New England pale to a peachy tan. It also made the freckles on her nose and cheeks darker and more plentiful. Someone probably got to have a hell of a time counting all of the new ones. *Someone...I wonder who is the lucky guy who gets to lick those freckles now...*

"Hello?" she asked, her tone icy. "After we get to the hospital, feel free to leave. Seems you were in a terrible hurry. Don't change your plans on my account." Fiona turned and nodded triumphantly from the front seat.

"No, I want to stay. Let me give you a ride back to your hotel."

"Oh, I don't need a ride. I'm going to stay at the hospital with Oba."

"Oba?"

"Yes, Oba." She pointed at the sleeping boy next to her.

"Oh! You know him?"

She pushed up her defiant, adorable little chin. "Yes. I know him. We just left this hospital a little over an hour ago after visiting with his very ill mother. She's dying, actually. That's why Oba ran into the street. He wanted to give her one last kiss."

Winston overheard and shook his head sadly as Andrew took a good look at Oba for the first time. The way he curled up so tightly next to Janet told him that they were very close. He could see that Janet was trying to be strong, but soon his façade began to crumble.

Tears filled her eyes as she whispered, "She knew she was dying and we didn't want Oba to witness it. Now we're back here and I have to tell him. I know he already knows, but I have to tell him."

"Oh, Janet…" He placed a hand on her back as she was getting out of the limo and into the wheelchair the nurse had at the curb. "I'm so sorry—"

Janet threw his hand off. "I'm fine." She swiped at tears on her cheeks. "*We* are going to be just fine. We don't need your pity."

"I'm sorry, Janet. If there's anything I can do—"

"Just get back in your SUV and drive out of my life. Let's start there."

As the door slammed shut, Winston clapped a supportive hand on Andrew's shoulder. "It's probably pointless to make a plea for you to keep your head on straight and stay focused on the business of acquiring this mine, right?"

Andrew gave his friend and colleague a stiff nod. As he watched the love of his life and that sweet little boy being wheeled into the hospital he knew one thing for sure. He would never be driven out of her life again.

CHAPTER FOUR: ALL MINES

Janet pulled the blankets up to Oba's chin and backed out of the room as quietly as she could. Ever since his mother's condition deteriorated, Oba had been staying at A Place for Grace. Gouta and Janet both agreed that it would make the inevitable transition much easier. Janet had given him a private room in the wing closest to her cottage. While she didn't want to seem to play favorites, she did tuck a few special things into his room, like a baseball lamp and a matching blanket. The boy loved to play ball.

It had taken hours to get him calmed down after they left the hospital. At five years old, Oba knew death. So many of his friends had lost their parents.

Although Gouta had done her best to shield her son from the harsh realities of the HIV crisis, not one soul in Africa was untouched. But no matter how much you understand death, you can never be prepared to lose the comfort of your mother. Especially when you're just a small boy.

"Is he sleeping?" Elyse Green asked.

"Finally," Janet said as she collapsed on the couch, grimacing when her arm banged against the cushion a little too hard.

Elyse was the youth counselor at A Place for Grace and she was probably the only person who got less sleep than Janet. Caring for the emotional and mental health of kids orphaned by HIV/AIDS was hard work, especially now that their occupancy had doubled due to the increase in children left orphaned.

"You should get some sleep, too," the older woman advised.

"Can't. I'm gonna crash here for a few hours, but I have to be at The Department of Mines at 9:30."

Elyse tsked. "Are they trying to expand the mines into the cemetery again?"

"Yes. There are diamonds out there. They'll eventually find someone with enough money to pay everyone off and proceed to desecrate those graves."

"But nothing has been done since that mine collapse two years ago."

"Of course not. They don't care about how it affects anyone. That's why I need to be there. No one ever talks about how The Department of Mines downplays the negative impact of the mining in Botswana. None of it makes the international news. The impact of mining on natural resources, vegetation, soil, bodies of water, and the human population aren't even recorded. If they did, the mining council would have to actually do something about it!" Janet felt herself getting angry again, and knew she wouldn't be able to sleep.

Janet knew the impact. She fed, clothed and wiped the tears of that very human impact every day.

Elyse walked across the room to drape a throw blanket over her.

"You can't save all of Botswana, Red."

Janet grunted in response and threw an arm over her tired eyes.

I might not be able to save all of Botswana, but I'm sure as hell going to try.

At 9:30 am sharp, with little more than a buttered

English muffin and strong coffee in her belly, Janet arrived at The Department of Mines, ready to do battle. She was meeting Radhika, A kindred spirit from Francistown who was determined to keep the cemetery intact. Some of Radhika's family members were buried there. She was a sort of community leader and mouthpiece for the indigenous people living in the area.

"Janet, it is so good to see you this morning. I heard about the accident. You are looking well."

Radhika's English was perfect as she strode across the lobby. Her style could best be described as Modern Traditional. Today she wore dark blue trousers with rust orange colored high-heeled boots under them. Because it was a business meeting, Janet supposed, Radhika's normally bold printed top was replaced with a more subdued turquoise blouse. The only compromise was a safari-inspired scarf wrapped around Radhika's long, elegant neck. Next to her, Janet felt frumpy, despite Elyse's assurance that she looked great today.

"I'm fine, Radhika. Come, sit here." The two of them had long since been banned from the inner offices, but they had no problem sitting quietly in the lobby to wait for Mykel Batou, Director of Banking and Economic Development to escort whatever CEO he was buttering up today. Today wasn't any different.

The women were catching up when Radhika's phone rang. She whispered, "I need to take this," and Janet could hear the clicking of her boots echoing through the lobby as she walked to a private area to take the call.

Resting her eyes for a moment, and now that the adrenaline and fatigue had worn off from the the previous day, Janet couldn't help but think of Andrew Atherton. His was the last face she expected to see in Botswana.

Last she heard Andrew had become the face of Atherton Diamonds. He had dabbled in modeling in college - mostly holiday ads for his parents, but when they graduated, he started modeling full-time for Atherton. In those days, Janet couldn't walk two blocks without seeing his steel blue eyes staring out at her from the side of a bus, or in storefront windows. Then there were the fashion shows and industry parties, and suddenly he was a part of the crowd that they loathed. The rich, beautiful and unaffected. A crowd she was born into, but never seemed to fit in.

Andrew's and Janet's families had different

missions in life. The Athertons were diamond miners — the very industry that was threatening the indigenous people Janet was here to protect. And Janet was the descendant of Stephen Girard, the wealthy philanthropist who'd donated his fortune to the education and welfare of orphans.

At first, Andrew and Janet's relationship was built on his rebellion from the family business. To him, modeling was a way to mock the family business. Yes, he would be a billionaire, but on his own terms.

But that started to change. The more Andrew rebelled, the harder his family clamped down. And dating a Girard was not part of their plan for him. The more they tightened their grip, the more he dived into the world of modeling and high fashion. Neither of those was Janet's scene, and that's why she left.

That glossy cover model was nothing like the boy she fell in love with. But he also wasn't the handsome rescuer who had lifted her into his arms last night. With that thick black hair and stubbly rough cheeks, this Andrew looked like some dashing billionaire version of Indiana Jones. He was broader and maybe even a little bit taller than the Andrew she knew. And damn sexy. She knew this from experience.

With Radhika still on the phone, Janet's mind continued to wander. What purpose could Andrew possibly have in Botswana? He must be on holiday. Maybe he bought one of those safari vacation packages that they are always pushing at the airport and hotel. Or a big game hunt, or whatever the ridiculously rich did when they came to Africa.

Either way, it was none of her concern. If last night was any indication, she would stay out of his way.

Janet was startled out of her reverie when she heard, "Here they come!" Radhika was elbowing Janet to get her attention.

They both stood and rushed to the other side of the the marble-floored lobby.

"Dumela, Mykel!" Radhika called out loudly. "And good morning to you!"

Mykel Batou sucked his teeth as he muttered to the man walking with him. "Pay no mind to these women…"

"Is this the businessman who wants to buy the land near the cemetery?"

"Cemetery? What cemetery?" the tall dark-skinned man with Mykel asked.

"Oh, he didn't tell you?" Janet asked. "So you don't know that where you want to dig is protected ancestral land? Or that there are tributaries on that land that feed into the Tati River? Or that building a mine there would destroy local vegetation, poison a water source and displace the people and the animals-"

"Is this true?" the man asked, looking at Mykel with a shocked expression on his face.

Janet squinted at him. He looked familiar. Where had she seen him before?

"Mr. Konteh, I assure you that The Department of Mines makes every effort to minimize exploitation-"

"Of the socio-economic and financial integrity during the the extraction and processing of precious minerals," Janet interrupted while rolling her eyes. "You're getting really good at that. Too bad you don't put some of that effort into safeguarding the health of your employees and minimizing the…"

Janet's words of protest died in her throat as another man strode up to the small group, piercing her with his steel blue eyes.

At the same time, each exclaimed, "Janet?" "Andrew?"

Andrew's brow furrowed and a nervous smile twitched at the corners of his mouth. "What are you doing here?"

"You know this woman?" Mykel asked.

Andrew's gaze traveled from her eyes and raked down the length of her body. Her eyes were blazing in anger, and her red curls looked like fire escaping from her head. He could almost feel the heat coming from her and was transfixed for a moment.

"Yeah," he said finally. "I know her."

"Well, maybe you can convince her to stop delaying or impeding progress on every mining permit that comes across my desk. You gentlemen have a great day. I'll be in touch." He strode away indignantly, leaving the rest of them staring at each other in the lobby.

"We have over fifteen hundred names on this petition!" Radhika shouted after him. "We will bring legal action if necessary!"

"Legal action" Andrew echoed, alarmed. 'What is all of this about, Red?"

"So that's why you're here? You're here to build a fucking mine?" Janet asked. "Are you here to dig up graves to get some damn diamonds?"

Andrew turned to his colleague, with his eyebrows raised, expecting an explanation.

Suddenly Janet recognized him. It was the man from the limo! Andrew's colleague.

"Don't look at me," the man said. "We were in the same meeting. I know as much as you do."

Andrew moved in close to Janet and dropped his voice. "If you know something, I need you to tell me, Red."

He was standing close enough for Janet to smell the hot cinnamon gum on his breath he liked to chew, and she could smell his sweat mingling with a clean, tangy citrus. It was a familiar scent that caused every nerve ending in her body to tingle. Oh, she remembered his spicy taste…

Janet clenched her teeth and attempted to steel herself before she looked up at him. "Where did he take you on your tour? To the gold mine? And then to some barren land full of scrub brush and told you that's where you're mine would be, right?"

"Are you implying that he showed us land that wasn't for sale?" Andrew's colleague asked.

"What's your name?"

"Winston Konteh," he said and his accent had a bit of Jamaican in it.

"Well, Mr. Konteh, that's exactly what I'm saying to you."

"How is that legal?" Winston was perplexed.

"It's not illegal. No money has been exchanged. At this point, it's all just talk." Janet could barely contain her anger.

Andrew turned and glared in the direction of Mykel Batou's office. Janet knew him well enough to know he was furious. No one tried to pull one over on Andrew Atherton. No one.

She could tell that he was debating whether he should stalk down the hall and give Mykel a beating. But instead, he looked at her and said, "Take me to the actual site for the new mine."

He then turned on his heels and strode past his waiting limo toward Janet's beat up old Land Rover.

CHAPTER FIVE: DIGGING UP THE PAST

Andrew seethed quietly as he rode in the passenger side of Janet's beat up old Land Cruiser to the real mining sites that he had flown halfway around the world to buy. He hated the fact that someone had attempted to con the big, dumb American for a fool. It was shit like this that made him reluctant to join the family business in the first place.

People had been surprised when his father named his sister Claudia as his successor. She wore the mantle of CEO and President of Atherton Diamonds well. It suited her, but the family business had never fit him. At least not until he was able to mold and carve his position into something he could stand doing every day. But that meant he had to try twice as hard to get everything right and this could have been a mistake that cost him billions of dollars.

That's billions with B.

The thought of it almost made him want to vomit.

"So this is what you're doing now? Prospecting for Atherton Diamonds?" Janet asked.

Andrew bristled. He wanted to have a serious conversation and he could sense that this could go sideways and he didn't want that to happen with Winston and Radhika in the backseat.

"Yeah," he answered finally. "When dad retired I had to step up and take a larger role. I couldn't stand the idea of being chained to a desk so I created a job that lets me work in the field."

She looked at him. Her light brown eyes caught the sunlight he was reminded of a weekend the spent at her family's home in the Hamptons. How he had spent the day kissing every inch of her on that private beach.

"What happened to the modeling?" she asked, a sardonic smile twitching at the corners of her mouth.

"I gave that up years ago. People didn't take me seriously. I got tired of being treated like an empty-headed pretty boy."

Janet scoffed. "Well, I'm glad that worked out for you," she said, though her tone said she was anything but.

"What about you? Have you been in Botswana all this time?"

She shifted her attention back to the road. "No. I spent some time in South America and Southeast Asia, but...Botswana has my heart. I volunteered here and decided that I wanted to open up orphanage here. Now I have three."

"Wow." There was really nothing more he could say about that. Janet had always been the nurturing type and had never met a worthy cause that she wouldn't get behind. "You really did it, huh?"

"Yeah, I really did."

They were outside of the city now and driving through one of the townships that skirted Francistown. The views were what one would expect to see in Africa with its sweeping landscapes and a sky so blue that it felt low enough that Andrew could reach up and touch it if he tried. In the distance, he could see a cemetery come into view. Janet pulled off the road and parked under the shade of some trees. The four of them got out, but Winston tapped him on the shoulder to get his attention.

"I want to go on record as saying that I'm not okay with desecrating graves. This kinda thing always comes back on you somehow."

"Comes back on you? What are you talking about? Karma?"

"Karma, payback, haunting, superstition, whatever you want to call it. I don't mess around with this kinda shit."

"Hm. I never took you for the superstitious type."

"Call me superstitious, but I don't mess around with shit like this," Winston repeated. "And you shouldn't either."

"Are you coming?" Janet called out from where she stood in the middle of the road. She looked adorable, like one of those girls that backpacked through Europe in her utilitarian pants, boots, and a t-shirt that looked soft and well worn. Radhika looked very out of place in this environment, but she was just as passionate as Janet about protecting the gravesite, so she kept up with Janet.

Winston tsked and fell in step alongside Andrew. Nodding his head toward Janet, Winston said, "Still say you need to keep away from that one, too, but you ain't listening."

"Nope. Not a chance."

They followed Janet through the cemetery skirting the graves. Andrew stayed close to and listened intently as she explained the customs of the Batswana people.

"Their an ancestral people meaning that the elderly and the deceased are revered. Most are Christian but still practice cultural rituals. they believe that the souls of the ancestors are close to them, close enough to hear their prayers and carry them to god."

"Modimo," Winston said, surprising Andrew.

"That's right," she said. "Modimo is a Supreme being. A creator and a director but he's not the sort of god that has time to intervene in the lives of the people who worship him."

"How do they…interact with these ancestors? Is there some sort of ceremony involved?"

"Ritual ceremonies occur around all of the major milestones of life; birth, death, coming of age. But they are also part of their everyday life so they talk to them daily."

"Hm. I can see why desecrating a cemetery would be disrespectful. Not that there is ever a respectful way to desecrate human remains, but…"

They arrived at the edge of the cemetery. The stand of trees continued for a few yards, but soon they were in the relentless midday sun. Andrew looked over at her and instantly began to worry about her fair skin. He moved a bit closer to her, positioning himself so that he stood between her and the sun, allowing her to walk in his shadow. She looked up at him. A strange expression came over her face.

"So what about this legal action?"

Radhika answered quickly. "The Department of Mines has offered a payout for the families that agree to have their relatives exhumed. But they won't pay up until all three-hundred and fifty families who have relatives buried here agree to accept it."

"I can imagine that has caused some discord in the community and within families as well," Winston said.

"Yeah, it would be a hard sell to get everyone to agree to exhume an entire cemetery."

"It definitely has caused problems in the community. And the worst part is that they don't even need to do it" Janet said as she tipped her chin toward a plot of land about three hundred yards away that was marked off with orange flags. "There's the mining site."

"But there's nothing else out there. There are ways to approach this dig without touching this cemetery,"

"Precisely, right. But they want to to go through the cemetery because digging there would be easier and they wouldn't have to build any roads."

"Is that what it's all about? Roads."

"No, it's really about money. The Department of Mines will always take the highest bidder, but will cut corners and do it as cheaply as possible."

Andrew had a look of contempt on his face as he folded his arms over his chest. "So how do I make this work? How do I get this mine and escape this corruption."

She sighed. "That's going to take a while to explain."

Walking a few steps ahead of Winston and Radhika, Andrew replied. "Okay, let me take you out to dinner so that we can talk about it. There has to be a middle ground and you seem like you're the person I need to talk to in order to make that happen."

Janet looked up at him warily. She wasn't the naïve type. Andrew could tell that she knew that dinner to discuss the mine was just a pretext to get her alone. But he also knew that this issue was something she felt passionate about and hoped that it would override whatever wariness she felt about being alone with him.

After looking him up and down skeptically, Janet

said, "Fine. I'll drop you back at your limo and you can meet me at Lila's Bistro at seven," she said then pivoted away from him to head back to the car. Andrew fell in step behind her unable to suppress his smile.

CHAPTER SIX: FRIENDS AND
BUTTERFLIES

Stepping into the shower, Janet could hardly believe that she agreed to have dinner with Andrew. *What was I thinking? We could have discussed the mine on the phone. Or in my office at least. This is a very, very bad idea.*

Yet, the entire time she was in the shower, Janet wasn't thinking about work. No cemeteries, no corruption, not even the orphanage. The warm soapy water running over her body as she washed reminded her of Andrew's hands. Those big, strong hands running over every curve of her body… exploring her dark places… No, her excitement over dinner was not for business. It was purely for pleasure.

As she was getting dressed, she tried to shake some sense into herself. "No, it's a business dinner.

That's all. I need to make sure he doesn't get caught up in the corruption. That's what any decent person would do for an old friend."

Andrew really was a good friend, too. She'd forgotten how much care and consideration he instinctively gave her-like walking next to her at just the right distance to keep the harsh, midday sun off of her face. Or how he listened intently to her thoughts and opinions and trusted them-trusted her. It had been a long time since she had a conversation with a man where she was treated with intelligence and respect instead of being treated like a meddling woman sent to inconvenience them.

In short, being around Andrew felt good and Janet denied herself of so many things that indulging in this one seemed harmless.

Grabbing her purse and keys, she stopped to kiss Oba goodnight. His little brown eyes were sleepy as he said, "You look pretty. Where are you going?"

"I'll be back soon, little king. I am just having dinner with a friend."

Lila's was within walking distance from Janet's place, and it was a lovely evening for a stroll, so she left the Land Cruiser at home. Janet had donned one of her three dresses - the one in forest green, and paired it with gold sandals, and some gold earrings she'd bought from a street vendor. Also, for the first time in a long time, she let her hair down. While her outfit wasn't 5th Avenue chic, she felt like she cleaned up nice, which was affirmed when she and Andrew locked eyes as she entered the bistro.

He stood to greet her, a slow appreciative smile spread across his lips. "Janet, you look great."

"Thank you…"

They fumbled through an awkward greeting- Andrew went in for a kiss and Janet thought they might hug which ended in a combination of both that made Andrew blush hard.

"Sorry, about that," he mumbled as he pulled out her chair.

"It's fine," she said tucking behind her ears, realizing that her face was probably beet red, too. She grinned and shook her head. "Why does this feel so awkward?"

"I ordered us a bottle of wine. Do you still drink chardonnay?"

Janet didn't want to let on that she hadn't been to dinner with a man in nearly three years, so she smiled and said, "Of course."

Andrew poured her a taste, and she nodded, and then he filled her glass before filling his own.

After a few minutes, the awkwardness subsided

and they fell back into the comfortable repartee from years ago. They caught up while they drank the first glass and surveyed the menu. Janet told him about her time in Southeast Asia where she had lived for several years after she left New York.

"I just needed to get away, you know? Far away from anything that looked or felt familiar or reminded me of home and-" She stopped short of saying what she was really running away from.

"Anything that reminded you of me," Andrew finished for her.

Janet didn't answer, but she really didn't need to; they both knew that what he said was true. "Either way, I needed to get away. I found myself and my real purpose when I left New York. I don't think I would have if I had stayed."

"How ironic. You found yourself during those years and I lost myself in ways I would have never predicted."

"Are you talking about the modeling and working with Atherton Diamonds? It seemed like you liked it."

"Hm." He drained his glass and took a moment to gather his thoughts while refilling it and topping hers off. "To be honest, I don't know if I liked modeling all that much. I did like the attention that came with it," he said honestly.

Janet always knew that was true, but it felt good to have that affirmed.

"Red…" He reached across the table and cover her hand with his. She looked up at him; met his earnest eyes. "I didn't treat you right in those last few days. you were right to leave the way you did. I just wish…"

Janet flipped her hand palm side up and laced her fingers through his. "I know what you mean." She stroked her thumb along his, a small, sad smile graced her lips. "For months after I left, I hoped you would just show up, engagement ring in hand, and an apology on your lips."

Andrew frowned, confused. "But no one knew where you were-"

"I didn't say the daydream made any sense," she said with a laugh. I just always hoped that you would come find and me and rescue me from myself and then you show up here."

"To be clear, I didn't rescue you. If anything, you rescued me. I almost killed you and that boy."

"But you're here. Of all the diamond mining sites in all of the world, you end up in Francistown. It could have been anywhere, but you're here." She gave his hand an affectionate squeeze. "You're here."

It seemed improbable that years of hurt could be

washed away with a simple exchange but Janet felt that some of it had.

They ate and drank another bottle of wine. As the evening progressed, their chairs moved closer and the smiles came easier until finally, it was time to pay the bill. Andrew paid the tab end offered to walk her home.

"So you live at the orphanage?" he asked.

They were on the sidewalk outside of the restaurant, Andrew maneuvered her to the inside, away from the street and tentatively took her hand.

"Yeah, I have a little cottage out back. It's cheaper and I'm still renovating and working out the particulars with this one. It presents a different range of problems. Sickness, war, displacement, all of that is at work here. It's a puzzle that is hard to solve, but I think that I'm getting close to a solution."

"And mining plays a big part in that."

"It does." She nodded but was reluctant to dig deeper. The night was so good. she didn't want to darken it with all the negative bits she fought to overcome every day. But on the other hand, he did ask her to dinner under the pretense of learning the particulars about the mining site. "What we really need is a mining company that makes a true effort to integrate into the community. The Department of Mines is supposed to facilitate that, but as I've explained they aren't too keen on doing that. In a perfect world, a portion of your proceeds would be invested into hospitals, schools, and the like."

"Are you receiving any funding from the local mines?"

"We had a little something going for a year or so with the company that runs the gold mine, but that fell through."

"So, how are you funding everything?"

"The Girard Foundation carries most of the weight, but my mother is always finding ways and reasons to make that difficult. I have a few really phenomenal brand ambassadors that raise money and collect shoes and clothing. We do all right, but we could always use more funding. "

Janet and Andrew were nearing the orphanage, and she found herself instinctively slowing down. She wasn't ready for the night to end.

"The site by the cemetery...its part of a land parcel that they have been trying to acquire for years now. I've helped in the fight to keep them from acquiring via imminent domain, but it's a struggle when so many people would benefit from the payout. Not only that...there aren't any other cemeteries close to here.

It would leave families without a place to lay their dead."

"Like that boy...the one you saved."

"Oba?"

"Yes, Oba. What's his story?"

"His mother's name was Gouta. We spent most of that day visiting his mother in the hospital. She's succumbing to the final stages and symptoms of AIDS. It's any day now, actually. Gouta came to us over a year ago. No family, no support system and a tiny boy to take care of. She signed over custody, but we allowed him to stay on with her while she was still well enough. She wanted him to have a home when she left this earth. Just recently, we moved him into A Place for Grace so that he wouldn't have to deal with the double trauma of losing his mother and his home."

"Wow," Andrew said simply. "I can't even imagine."

"Anyway. I have a soft spot for that kid. I try really hard not to get attached, but there's something about this little boy."

"He's pretty cute, so that's totally understandable. Will his mother be buried in that cemetery?"

Janet nodded. "More than likely, yes. We're gathering the funds to give her a proper burial now."

"I'd like to contribute," he said. "In any way I can. How is Oba doing?"

Janet shook her head. "Not great. But we're doing what we can to help him grieve. I know from experience that the funeral is going to be the hardest part for him."

He squeezed her hand. "He's lucky to have you to help him through this."

"I hope I'm enough," she said. "Sometimes I wonder if I'm doing the right thing with the little ones like Oba."

"Have you ever thought about adopting any of them?"

"I have, but not right now. Maybe when I'm a little older and a little more settled. I want to be able to give a kid a real family. Most of them have already gone through so much before they even get here, that I don't want to add more problems."

"I don't know, Red. You've always been a nurturing soul. I think you will make a great mother."

She looked up at him and smiled. "Thank you for saying that."

"It's the truth," he said with a shrug.

"Well, here we are," she said. Janet turned to face him at the foot of the orphanage's stairs and was surprised to find that she wasn't ready to say goodnight. "Do you want to come in for a cup of coffee or tea? The kids are probably getting ready for bed, but I could give you a tour."

"Can I take a raincheck?" he asked. "I want to get back to my hotel and talk to Claudia about all of this. She's establishing a relationship with a friend of ours that's an investor and I want to see how much of this we can make happen."

"Right. Of course," she said with a nod. "Actually...I have a new group of volunteers coming in tomorrow to help paint some newly renovated rooms and set up bunks and bureaus for the kids. One of them is actually an old friend of mine - a magazine publisher who is doing a write-up on A Place for Grace. Why don't you stop by then?"

"An old friend, huh? Do I need to bring my boxing gloves?" Andrew smiled.

"Hahaha, no, it's a woman. Nicole."

"Oh, okay then. I'll definitely be there. Is it alright if I bring Winston along?"

"Sure. We need all of the help we can get."

"Okay, then. It's a date." Andrew smiled at Janet. "We had a good time tonight," he said. It wasn't a question. It was a statement. A statement that she couldn't help but agree with.

"Yes, we did," she said with a smile.

"I don't want to fumble my way through a goodbye that will probably be as awkward as our hello so, I'll settle for this."

He brought the hand that he was holding to his lips and gave each of her knuckles a sweet kiss. It shouldn't have affected her, but those sweet kisses sent a thrill through her as if he'd brushed his lips across her lips instead of the back of her hand.

"Goodnight, Janet."

"Goodnight, Andrew." With warm cheeks and belly full of butterflies, she went inside.

CHAPTER SEVEN: ONCE BITTEN, TWICE SHY

"So how are things going over there?" Claudia asked.

Andrew had spent several hours "working" (really daydreaming about his dinner with Janet) when he suddenly remembered that New York was seven hours behind Francistown. Luckily, it was early evening in New York and Andrew had caught his sister just as she came in from the office.

"Things are going pretty well. Winston and I toured a couple of mining sites in the area and we've narrowed it down to one of two." For some reason, Andrew didn't want to mention the issue with the Department of Mines just yet.

"Wow, that was fast. But that's good. Real good."

"How're things going with Cole?"

Cole had been Andrew's roommate in college and was actually Claudia's fiancé. But Andrew wasn't referring to their personal relationship. Cole was also deciding on whether or not to invest in Atherton Diamonds, and without the infusion of his capital, it would be very difficult for Atherton to purchase one mine, let alone buy the land around it. In other words, Cole's decision to invest in the company would make or break this deal.

"He's a bit..." Claudia paused for a moment. "Unconventional," she said finally. "But I guess things are going all right."

Andrew nodded. "Good, good. You know how you guys are. Just keep working on him." Then casually, ever so casually, Andrew mentioned, "Hey, you'll never guess who I ran into over here."

Claudia sounded confused and slightly suspicious of her brother's overly casual tone. "Ran into? It's Botswana. Who could you have possibly run into in Botswana?"

"Janet."

"Janet?" Claudia sounded shocked.

"Yep." Andrew could practically see the look on his sister's face right now.

"Janet Girard?"

"Yeah, she lives here in Botswana. She runs an orphanage out here."

Claudia groaned. "Of course she does. So did you let her have it? Did you demand to know why she disappeared without a word?" She sounded angry, but then again, she also watched her brother fall apart from the heartbreak.

"No, I didn't let her have it. But I did take her out to dinner and apologize for how I treated her."

"*You* apologized to *her*? What for? She left you! You were a wreck when she left. You got a DUI, you were splattered across all of the gossip blogs and tabloids-"

"Yes, I was a wreck, but she was right to leave. I turned into one of those rich dirtbags and I lost sight of the things that were important to me. Janet was one of those things."

"Sounds like a convenient excuse if you ask me. So, what did you talk about? Are you going to adopt an orphan or something?" Claudia still had a tone, but it was softening.

"She actually knows a lot about how things work over here." He broke into an amused smile. "She actually showed up at the Department of Mines to confront the officials and revealed some unethical practices-"

"Wait. She's involved in this mining deal?"

"Only peripherally. The site we're most interested in is near a cemetery. Department of Mines wants to pay all of the families and exhume the bodies-"

"That's awful."

"Yeah, you have no idea. But I think that if we put our heads together, we can come up with a way for us to purchase the mining site, keep the cemetery intact, and make a positive impact on the surrounding provinces. But we're going to need a lot more money, so see if you can't patch things up with Cole along as quickly as possible."

Claudia rolled her eyes again. "You say that as if you think I'm hindering this process in some way."

"Well...I didn't mean it that way at all. Defensive much? "Andrew smiled because this was the way he and his sister talked. They were always honest with each other.

"He's just...unconventional, but I will try to move things along."

"Good. I'll send you the details as soon as we get it all down on paper."

"I'll keep an eye out for it. One other thing...Andrew?"

"Yeah, sis?"

"Just...be careful. It sounds like you and Janet have come to some sort of understanding, but be careful. Once bitten, twice shy and all of that."

"Okay, sis. I will."

The next morning during a long hard run on the treadmill in the hotel gym, Andrew considered the fact that both his sister and his good friend Winston had warned him against getting tangled up with Janet again. *Who knows? Maybe they are right. Maybe she'll run off again and break my heart.*

But Janet seemed different to that temperamental redhead he knew in college. She seemed centered and more mature. Andrew knew that he had matured a lot in the years they spent apart. He was ready to settle down and start a family.

Pulling on his jeans he couldn't help but laugh at that thought. "Who would have ever imagined me, Andrew Atherton, thinking of settling down and getting married..."

Walking into the hotel restaurant, Winston and Fiona were already at the table. They were having breakfast to go over the specifics for the mine purchase.

Moving the salt and pepper shakers aside, Winston unrolled a map. "I got this from the girl at the front desk. It's completely different than the one the official gave us yesterday."

"Wait...you've already been to the Department of Mines this morning?"

"No..." Winston said with a sly smile. "She delivered it yesterday evening."

"I see," Andrew said with a knowing raise of his brows.

"Anyway, can we get our minds back on our business?" Fiona complained.

"Right, so this is the parcel of land they want to sell us and here's the cemetery," Winston pointed out. "But there's also this adjacent parcel over here."

"Yeah, Janet mentioned that. She said that we would have to buy both in order to leave the cemetery untouched."

"And you think the Department of Mines would allow that?" Fiona asked. "They went out of their way to hide the fact that they planned to exhume those bodies and raze the cemetery."

"True," Winston agreed. 'And what about the families? The ones who want to exhume for the money? Are we going to pay them off?"

"No...that wouldn't make sense fiscally. Besides, isn't it their job to make sure they hire from within the community?" Andrew asked.

"I've looked into it, but I haven't been able to find any community initiatives," Fiona said after taking a sip of her coffee. "They only seem to hire unskilled workers locally and don't do much locally to get the people in the neighboring provinces more training."

"But can't we make that our focus? When we open the mine? Just because things have always been done this way doesn't mean it is the only way to get things done," Andrew said.

Winston nodded. "You're right."

Fiona gathered up her things. "I'll get started on the necessary paperwork," she said as she stood up. "Oh! I saw that you blocked out most of the morning with a visit to A Place for Grace. Do you need me for that or…?"

"No. I'm volunteering a few of hours to help Janet and her staff set up some bunks and stuff. I could use your help, Winston. If you don't have anything planned."

"You mean like manual labor?" Winston asked for clarification.

'Yeah. Have you suddenly became too precious to get your hands dirty?"

Winston scoffed. "What time are we leaving?"

CHAPTER EIGHT: THAT GIRL

Janet's morning started even earlier than usual. The delivery trucks were coming at 7:00 am to drop off boxes containing fifty new bunk beds and bureaus. And, before they could be assembled, there were three newly renovated rooms that needed a fresh coat of paint. Janet and Elyse had moved all of the furniture out of the rooms the day before, but there was still a lot to do before the trucks arrived. And the ten volunteers - twelve with Andrew and Winston - were due to arrive at 6:45 am.

She didn't run A Place for Grace like most of the orphanages she had volunteered at over the years; meaning she didn't have a constant stream of volunteers. While it was nice to have the help, her main goal was to maintain consistency and stability for the kids at Grace and that was hard to do with a constant stream of volunteers coming and going. However, it was difficult to get things done without the free and steady support - even with The Girard Foundation footing most of the bill. Her mother was constantly tightening those purse strings as if Janet's requests were frivolous.

That's why Janet's best friend from New York had flown into volunteer. Not only was Nicole Burns Janet's oldest friend, she was also the head of Straw Barn Publishing. She was here to do a profile on A Place for Grace that would appear in several of Straw Barn's publications. There would be magazine and newspaper coverage, as well as a YouTube documentary. The idea was that generating publicity would help raise awareness - and funds. Plus, Janet and Nicole hadn't seen each other in a couple of years, and it was definitely time for a reunion. Even if it did mean assembling furniture as an excuse to get together.

The dining hall was packed with kids gobbling down their breakfasts before heading off to school. The clang of metal utensils and boisterous voices of the children were some of Janet's favorite sounds on the planet. Happy, normal children sounds.

Except there was one sad-looking little boy sitting alone at the end of a long wooden table. It was Oba, and he was pushing some scrambled eggs around on his plate with a fork. Janet grabbed a bowl of cornflakes and a banana. She took them and her coffee over to sit down beside him.

"Good morning, little king," she said cheerily as she peeled the banana and sliced half of it into her bowl before giving Oba the other half. He pushed his plate away and nibbled on it and at this point, seeing him eat half of a banana was almost as good as a smile.

"Do I have to go to school today?" he asked.

"Of course! All little kings need schooling so that they can become wise, big kings. What's wrong?"

"I miss mama." Oba's eyes brimmed with tears.

"Oh, honey. I know you do. But if you go to school you might just forget how much you miss her…just for a little while."

"Can't I stay with you? Just for today, I promise. I won't be in the way. Tomorrow I will go back to school and be happy. Just one day. Please?"

Janet couldn't resist his little face.

"I know you're sad, Oba, but going to school might be just the thing to not be sad for a little while."

"I know, but...can't I just stay here?" He put down the half-finished banana and leaned against her.

"Okay, Oba. You can stay today, but you're going to have to help me. I have lots of hard work to do."

"Don't worry, Oba," said a familiar deep voice. "We'll help you with some of that hard work."

Janet looked up to see Andrew standing over her. The smile that spread across her face was bright and involuntary.

"But you're gonna have to use your muscles," Winston said before flexing his biceps. "My mate Andrew and I don't hang around with slackers. You're gonna have to pull your weight. All right, Oba?"

Oba sat up straight and proud as if to show he were a man, too. He nodded. "Alright."

"I can't believe how good it is to see you again!" Janet hugged Nicole tightly.

Nicole's bouncy blond curls swung as she shook her head from side to side. "I can't believe you aren't aging. What is in this African water? And where can I get some?" Nicole laughed.

"I'm glad you brought your camera and notepad. I

can't tell you how much I appreciate you being here to help. It's not really a big thing - just some furniture. But bringing attention to A Place for Grace will help shine a light on how many kids are in need over here."

"Well, I'm here to help, too. Don't be fooled by this dainty exterior. I'm like one of those mints in a can. I'm 'curiously strong'" Nicole flexed her non-existent biceps at that statement as Janet laughed.

Elyse and Janet conducted a brief orientation and they split up the group: some to paint the newly-renovated rooms and the rest to assemble the bunks and bureaus. Winston and Andrew ended up in Janet's group. Together they unloaded the truck full of flat-packed furniture. Oba helped them tear into the boxes and kept track of all of the screws, washers and lug nuts.

It was fun for Janet to work shoulder to shoulder with Andrew again. It reminded her of those summers when they volunteered for Habitat for Humanity.

By lunchtime, they had seventeen of the bunks assembled and just about the same amount of bureaus stood between them. Getting those put together was a little bit slower because it was a two-man job.

Janet invited Winston and Andrew back to the cottage for lunch. She'd invited Nicole, too, but she wanted to take some notes while the morning was still fresh in her mind. Winston begged off too - apparently, he had a lunch date. So it was Andrew, Oba, and Janet in the kitchen of her tiny, two bedroom cottage.

Andrew was sweaty. His dark curls clung to his forehead and the nape of his neck. Janet grabbed two bottles of water while she made the sandwiches, and gave them to Andrew and Oba.

"Thank you," he murmured before twisting off the top and drinking the whole bottle in one swig.

Oba's big brown eyes watched Andrew, and then he parroted, "Thank you," and opened the top of the bottle before trying to drink the whole thing like Andrew had. Unfortunately, his five-year-old throat was too small, and Oba started coughing and sputtering water.

It went all over Andrew's white t-shirt, and Oba was terrified that Andrew would be angry. His eyes filled with tears. "I'm sorry I got your shirt wet. I didn't mean it."

"Slow down there, little man," Andrew said with a chuckle as he reached for a dry dish towel to clean off

Oba's face and shirt. "It's not a big deal at all. Shirts can be replaced. People cannot."

With that, Andrew grabbed the bottom of his wet t-shirt and pulled it over his head, revealing the rippled muscles that Janet remembered so well.

Janet's cheeks flushed bright pink as he used the shirt to mop up a droplet of sweat making its way down the middle of his chest. The man hadn't gained an ounce of fat in a decade. He was as fit as ever.

His eyes met hers and it was clear that he had noticed her noticing. With a roll of her eyes and a slight smile, she took his shirt out onto the porch and left it to dry.

"How about we have a contest to see who can eat the most of their sandwich? But, it's not a race. We don't want any more choking, do we, Oba?"

Oba smiled and picked up one half of his sandwich. With a bite full, Oba said, "I'm going to win!"

Watching Andrew and Oba laughing and talking and eating around her kitchen table warmed Janet's heart. It felt like the most natural thing in the world. The boy she loved and the man she... What did she feel for Andrew? She couldn't help but wonder what it would be like if this were her family.

. . .

After their sandwiches of leftover roast beef and thick homemade bread, Oba was declared the winner of the contest. Janet was secretly impressed that Andrew had gotten Oba to eat his whole sandwich. And her heart was warmed when she saw he'd left a little bite on the plate so that Oba could "win."

Setting a plate of chocolate chip cookies down on the table, Janet asked, "So did you get a chance to talk to your sister?"

"I did. She's on board with buying both parcels as long as I can get the community element without encountering a ton of red tape. Do you know who I contact about that? Any organizers who know exactly what the people need?"

"Of course! I'll get you a list of names."

"While on my run this morning, I thought of some ambassadors I can hook you up with back in London."

"That would be super helpful. Thanks for doing that."

"No need to thank me. You're helping me out so of course, I want to do what I can to help you, too."

Janet smiled at him and for a moment, she allowed herself to think of how it would be if they were truly partners, if they were still together and supporting each other in this way. She's been doing it alone for so long that the thought of having someone help her navigate all of this nearly brought her to tears.

Andrew reached out and touched her arm. "You got real quiet all of a sudden. Are you alright?"

She nodded. "It just feels good to have someone help me without all of the begging. Whenever I need money or funding for A Place for Grace it always requires some level of groveling, even when I go to my mother. It's just refreshing, that's all."

"I'm sorry that you feel so alone in all of this. I wish I could do more."

"You're doing more than enough. And I will thank you properly with a drink of the alcoholic variety when we're done building all of these bureaus and bunks!"

It took much longer than anticipated to get all of the bunks and bureaus assembled. The kids were asleep and most of the volunteers agreed to head down to the local bar to drink away the aches and pains of the day. As expected, Nicole had some work to do at the hotel and couldn't join them. Janet and Andrew went and bought the first round.

With a few drinks in her and so many hours

working closely with him, she felt brave enough to ask the question she'd been dying to ask.

Janet leaned her elbows on the table and looked him in the eye. "Tell me the truth. Were you ever really in love with me?"

His eyes widened with surprise. "What a question!" he said. "Do you really doubt that I did? When I told Claudia that I'd run into you - literally - she proceeded to remind me of the DUI and all the tabloid and gossip drama that I brought on myself in the months after you left."

"Oh, so...all of those drunken antics were because I left? Is that what you're saying? You didn't look all that lonely."

Andrew looked into his glass. "I was. There may have been women in my bed, but I was very lonely." He sighed and leaned his elbows on the table, bringing their faces within inches of each other. "Now, let me ask you the same question. You left without a goodbye or a forwarding address. Did you ever love me?"

"I loved you more than I loved myself. I saw that I was willing to change who I was. To make sacrifices that I would have never considered just to be near you."

"You saw yourself becoming your mother," he said.

"Right." Janet's mother Alexis had always been jealous of her. Janet never really understood why. Alexis was gorgeous, smart, funny and married to a successful businessman. Why she felt the need to intrude on Janet's life at every turn, play power and guilt trips, and basically make Janet's life difficult was something beyond comprehension.

Alexis had sacrificed everything when she got unexpectedly pregnant and married Janet's father. She'd given up everything that mattered to her, and Janet felt the same thing happening during those years with Andrew. She never wanted to end up bitter and angry like her mother.

"Dad made her give up so many of her career goals. And she resents me for it," Janet said, sighing deeply.

"I would have never done that to you. Your dreams and goals are too important to you — and to the world. To ask you to give up your passion…" Andrew shook his head as if to drive away the thought.

"But…" The tears started to flow down Janet's freckled cheeks.

Andrew tenderly wiped them away, repeating, "I would have *never* done that to you, Red. And I would've never let you do that to yourself."

Ugh. She was that girl. That drunk girl at the bar, and crying while her boyfriend tried to console her. Except she wasn't a girl anymore. She was a grown woman almost in her thirties and he wasn't her boyfriend. *Just a good friend*, she thought, as she closed the distance between them giving him a shy, tentative kiss.

He didn't return the kiss at first. Maybe it was shock, or maybe he wasn't interested, but whatever it was, his hesitance stole her bravado.

"I'm sorry," she murmured as she pulled away. "I shouldn't have-"

"Don't you dare," Andrew all but growled then took her face in both of his hands and kissed her thoroughly.

Oh, god. Now she was that girl kissing her ex-boyfriend in a bar, but she was too electrified to care. Every place on her body that he had ever kissed or touched remembered the feel of his mouth and hands. It was all she could do to stay on her side of the table and not crawl into his lap.

"Damn, Red," he whispered. "We've been drinking. We should not be doing this, but god...I really don't want to stop kissing you." Andrew captured her mouth again. Tongue plunging into her mouth, hot and searching, making her forget that she ever had inhibitions.

"Mmm…" he moaned as he pulled away again. "We're both a little drunk. I should get you home. But I strongly suggest that we resume this again when we're both sober. Let me settle up this bill."

Janet watched him walk toward the bar. She respected the fact that he wanted to revisit this when they were sober and clear-headed. But part of her wished that he wasn't such a gentleman and would take her back to her cottage and make love to her.

CHAPTER NINE: SEAL THE DEAL

He was done for.

Andrew had been reliving that kiss in the bar all night after he dropped her off at the orphanage. He knew that he had done the good and noble thing by taking her home but his body didn't agree. He'd spent a considerable amount of time in the shower trying to alleviate the need that those kisses had inspired. After a hard run and a slow rub and tug, he came to one conclusion:

He was still in love with Janet.

And while that kiss in the bar, the one on the street corner while they waited for the light, and the ones on her doorstep were amazing, he didn't want to take this a step further until he knew they were on the same page.

Ding. It was a text message from Janet. "Good morning, handsome. You up?"

Laughing, he typed back. "Always."

"Last night was amazing. I can't stop smiling."

Andrew was delighted to see that she was happy about the kisses. He was afraid it would be a block of text detailing why it had been a mistake. Instead, here they were flirting.

Ding. "I have what you need. You know, what I promised you last night?"

Oh, this was fun. "Is that so? When can I have it?"

He laughed when she texted back the names and contact information of the community leaders he could talk to. He forwarded that one part to Fiona. Carefully.

"Will I see you later, Red?"

"I hope so. Can you come by after your morning meeting?"

"I wouldn't miss it for the world."

Andrew, Winston, and Fiona had a meeting at the Department of Mines at 9:00 am. Fiona had the paperwork squared away and they were going over the documents before a 9:30 with Mykel Batou. He was still unsure about Cole and the financing, but he had to keep things moving forward.

In the car on the way there, Andrew's phone rang. It was Claudia's ringtone.

"Sis'? Is everything okay? It's late over there."

"Yes! Everything is okay. Better than okay." Claudia's normally composed demeanor was replaced with an almost giddy flush to her voice. "We have the financing. Cole signed the investment papers tonight!"

Andrew did a fist pump. "Yes! Way to go Claudia. He won't be sorry. This investment is going to pay off. Not only in terms of money, but in helping a community that really needs it. Thank you so much."

"Now, you go seal the deal at the Department of Mines."

Cole and Claudia had worked out the investment end of things in New York. All systems were a go. The meeting was just a formality.

Fiona was waiting in the lobby of The Department of Mines with the paperwork in-hand and a cup of coffee for Andrew.

"I heard you had quite the night. I figured that you may need this."

"Good news travels fast. Are these the documents?"

"Yup. You know the drill. Sign and initial next to the tabs."

"Gotcha." he took the pen from her and proceeded to apply his John Hancock where it was required. "Did you contact the list of community leaders I sent you?" he asked as he scribbled away.

"Yes. I'll call Janet and see if we can set up a meeting this evening."

"Good. That's great."

Fiona sipped at her coffee, then leaned in close to him. "Can I say something?"

Andrew cut his eyes at her. "You're asking to speak your mind? Since when is that a thing?"

"I have no problem talking to you about business related stuff, but…"

"This is about Janet," he finished for her.

"Yeah, you two have history."

"We do."

"I'm gonna say this and you can take it or leave it, but I think you need to be careful about involving an ex in your business dealings. Most exes are exes for a reason."

"Fiona, I really appreciate your concern, but…"

"Am I late?" Winston asked as he jogged up.

Fiona looked irritatedly at her phone as Andrew stood to greet his friend.

Winston looked at the cups in hers and Andrew's hands and said jokingly, "You didn't bring me a cup of coffee?"

"I'm his assistant. Not yours," she said with a shrug. "Besides. You're late."

"Mr. Atherton? Mr. Konteh?" the receptionist called out. "Mr. Batou is ready to see you now."

"Well," Andrew said. "Let's get this over with." Fiona stepped aside to make the call to Janet while Winston and Andrew went through the glass doors to the offices.

Mykel Batou was more pleasant and forthcoming than he had been at previous meetings. He was more than happy to facilitate the purchase of both mining sites and didn't even question what would happen to the cemetery or where Andrew got the information that they could buy both parcels from. He simply took their signed contracts, initiated the transfer of funds and shook their hands.

"It was a pleasure doing business with you," Mr. Batou said.

It was disturbingly easy, but Andrew didn't dwell

on it because it meant that he could go to the orphanage for lunch.

"I guess he really only wanted the money," Winston commented as they walked out the front door of the building. "No concern for the people at all."

"I've always found that in business, compassion is more rare than diamonds, my friend."

CHAPTER TEN: DEJA VU

"Good morning, A Place for Grace. This is Janet."

"Janet, hi, it's Fiona. Andrew's assistant?" Her voice was artificially sweet.

"Oh hi. Nice to hear from you. What can I do for you?"

"This morning over coffee, Andrew showed me the text you sent with the names of the community leaders you wanted him to contact. We called them, and we were wondering if you could join us at our hotel for a meeting."

Our hotel? He showed her the text? The one she sent when he was in bed? What was Fiona doing in his bed? Visions of them in bed, drinking coffee and making those calls made her nauseous. Her head started to spin. He *was* a little drunk. Maybe all that kissing got him too turned on, and he knocked on Fiona's door at the hotel, and…

"Well?" Fiona sounded impatient.

"Why don't we all meet here. For dinner. At my cottage. 6:30." At least if she were going to see them together, she could do it on her own turf. Hitting the "end" button a little too hard, Janet struggled to focus on her work while her stomach churned.

Composing a text to Andrew, Janet wrote, "Too busy for lunch today. Don't come by. See you and Fiona at dinner." Tears in her eyes, the words blurred, as she hit "Send."

"Can I come to dinner and see Mr. Andrew too?" Oba looked up at Janet with those big, pleading eyes. "I won't spill anything."

"No, little king. This is a business meeting. Mr. Andrew will be leaving soon after he finishes his business here. But I'll come back and give you a kiss goodnight. Okay, Oba?"

Janet's heart was heavy. All of her fantasies about Andrew and getting back together were just that. Fantasy. He was the same playboy she knew from college.

"And so here is a list of things we intend to do for the community, now that we have the parcels that surround the cemetery." Fiona passed out a list to each of the leaders that sat around Janet's small table.

"I wanted to meet with you all at once so that we could decide together what is best for the community."

Andrew kept trying to catch Janet's eye with furtive glances and smiles, but she avoided his glance. *Just get through the dinner and he will leave and you'll never have to see him again. You can do this.*

Fiona was really putting on a show for Janet, too. Leaning over Andrew's shoulder as she pointed to something on the list. Refilling his iced tea whenever he took more than three sips. It was clear there was something going on between them, even though Andrew was pretending there wasn't.

"There are a lot of things that Atherton Diamonds can provide for the community on the land surrounding the mine — schools, hospitals with special accommodations for patients with HIV/AIDS where they can receive the best and latest treatment. We also want to build a place where families can be together during long hospital treatments." Andrew looked at Janet, as if for approval, but she just looked away.

He's just using his money to try and get me into bed. I'm not falling for it. I'm not that girl.

As the meeting drew to an end, and everyone was trickling out the door, Andrew caught Janet's arm. "Hey. I haven't talked to you all night. I missed you today."

"Did you?" Janet couldn't stop the tone from seeping into her voice. "I was busy today. Sorry."

"Are you upset with me, Red? Did I do something?" His face looked crestfallen.

He was so clueless.

"You could say that. Listen, I promised Oba I'd tuck him into bed. I need to go. Good luck at your final meeting with Mykel tomorrow."

Leaving him with a confused look on his face, Janet turned and walked out her own front door, swinging her red ponytail behind her.

CHAPTER ELEVEN: BETRAYED

"I do not understand women, Winston. At all." It was 11:00 pm and Andrew was running his frustration off at the hotel gym. Winston was seated near him, texting someone on the phone.

"They are mysterious creatures, mate. That's for sure."

"I mean, one minute Janet and I are flirting and making plans to see each other, and then the next minute she's ice cold to me." He turned the speed up on the treadmill. "I don't even know what I did!"

Just then, Andrew's phone began to ring. It was Claudia's tone. Andrew hit "stop" on the treadmill and answered the phone. "Claudia? It's the middle of the day there. Is something wrong?"

Her voice sounded stressed. "You could say that. It's this mining deal. It's falling apart."

"What do you mean? We signed the papers yesterday. Fiona wired the deposit this morning. I'm just going in in the morning to pick up the confirmed copies."

"That's what I thought too. I got a call this afternoon from a business friend of mine. That Mykel Batou? He's crooked. Those papers you signed were fake. He took our money and still owns the land."

Andrew was blinded with rage. "What the hell?" He ended the call abruptly. "I'll get to the bottom of this and call you back."

Winston, who had only overheard Andrew's side of the conversation, looked up, shocked. "What is going on?"

At that moment, Winston's phone buzzed. "Yes? Wait, what? They're where? Oh my god. Thank you for calling. We'll be right there.

"Andrew. That was…a friend of mine. She called to tell me that there are bulldozers right now down at the cemetery. They are going to raze the grounds in the middle of the night! We need to get over there."

The lights could be seen from a mile away. The Department of Mines had set up huge focus lights that illuminated the entire cemetery. As Andrew sped down the winding roads that led there, his heart pounded with fury. "I can't believe he did this. He stole our money and is now going to desecrate graves that have been here for hundreds of years. Under the cover of darkness, no less. How can someone be that disgusting?"

Winston answered as he texted. "They'll get their karma. Don't you worry."

Andrew's hands gripped on the steering wheel as he replied, "It will be sooner rather than later if I have my way."

Dust flying in the dark, Andrew and Winston screeched up to the dirt lot next to the grave site. To his surprise, Janet's friend Radhika stepped out from the shadows and into the beam of light from the headlights, and headed toward them.

"This is your friend?" Andrew looked at Winston. "This is who you've been seeing in town?"

Winston grinned and looked down as he unbuckled his seat belt. "We can talk about that later. We have some destruction to stop."

Radhika and Winston embraced briefly and then headed toward the cluster of lights and bulldozers. Andrew sat in shock for a moment before he heard his friend say, "Come on mate. We need to hurry."

Andrew was still wearing his athletic clothes, and

so he took off in a sprint toward the site. As he got near, he saw what could best be described as a stand-off. On one side of the graves were a group of a dozen or so construction workers, wearing hard hats and standing in front of looming bulldozers. Facing them in a human chain that made a perimeter around the entire cemetery was a huge group of, probably 10,000 locals. Nearly a tenth of Francistown's entire population had come out to protect the graves.

As he approached the group, he saw Mykel standing near one of the construction workers. He was still wearing a suit. *Who wears a suit at midnight?* Andrew couldn't help but wonder.

"What the hell is going on here?" Andrew stormed up to Mykel, whose eyes widened in fear.

"We are performing within our legal rights, Mr. Atherton. I'm afraid there was an error on the paperwork you signed, and we are still in ownership of this land. Please step aside, or I will have you arrested."

Eyes blazing in fury, Andrew grabbed Mykel by his collar. "You are right that there has been a mistake. But the mistake was you thinking that you could get away with this. You have NO idea who you are dealing with. Zero. My family has been in the mining business for more than two hundred years. Do you know what that means, MYKEL?" Andrew was so close to him that his name had come out like a bark.

Mykel, whose throat was still in Andrew's grip, tried to swallow as he shook his head.

"It means that we have a lot of friends. Friends in high places. And we also have friends in low places. Very low places. Do you know what I mean by that?" The last part of the sentence came out as a menacing whisper.

Mykel's forehead was beading with sweat.

"This is what is going to happen. Listen very closely to what I say, because I will not repeat myself. You are going to call off those bulldozers. They are NOT going to be tearing up the graves of these people. Not tonight. Not ever. You will not dishonor their ancestors like this. Do you understand so far?"

Mykel nodded yes.

"Then, I am going to arrive at your office at 9:00 sharp, and you will have legal versions of the paperwork I signed yesterday. If I find out that you pulled any more bullshit, you will be very, very sorry. Your career will be over, to say the least. Your government will face decades of legal battles. And, more importantly, you will never get a good night's sleep again because you will never know when one of my *friends* will come to your door in the middle of the night." He released Mykel's throat. "Got it?"

"Yes." Mykel was rubbing his neck where his shirt had been choking him from Andrew's grasp.

"Oh, and one other thing. The Department of Mines will pay for the headstones for every family who needs one for the next five years."

Before he could hear Mykel's response, Andrew turned and walked away. Passing Winston and Radhika, he simply said, "We're good here. See you in the morning."

CHAPTER TWELVE: COMING TOGETHER

Janet popped open the top of another beer and handed it to her friend David while he was regaling the group with the story of what had happened last night at the cemetery.

"There must have been fifty thousand people there!" David said, gesturing his hands wide.

Janet laughed as she sat down at her dining room table. "Really, David? We all know you have a tendency to exaggerate."

It had been a while since Janet had hosted a dinner with the women who had befriended her when she first moved to Botswana. Although David was not a woman, his flamboyant personality made him a welcome addition to the group.

They still met for the occasional beer and ranting session, but whenever they came together like this, around her kitchen table, Janet couldn't help but feel warm, fuzzy feelings of family that made her wonder why she didn't do it more often. *These are my real friends*, she thought as she looked around the table at Elyse, Radhika, David and Coral, a local teacher.

"Speaking of last night," David lowered his voice to a gossipy whisper, as he turned to Radhika, "are you going to tell them who I saw you kissing in the shadows last night, or shall I?" He had a mischievous smile on his face.

Radhika's ebony skin flushed a little as she grinned. "I think we have more important things to talk about. Like how Andrew saved the cemetery."

The deflection didn't work. David blurted out, "It was Winston! That is who Radhika has been sneaking off to see!"

The women's faces lit up with happy surprise. "Winston! Radhika, why didn't you say anything?" "Sister, he is seriously handsome." "And that accent!" They all chimed in.

Radhika commented softly. "I didn't say anything because I'm not sure if it's going anywhere. He doesn't live in Botswana, as you know. But, I do really like him…"

The other women and David just nodded and started talking about how Winston and Radhika could be together. But, Janet's mind started to wander as she thought of Andrew.

Radhika had told her how Andrew stormed down to the cemetery and confronted Mykel. They had been trying to get the upper hand on Mykel for months, and somehow Andrew accomplished it in a matter of minutes.

Janet's heart started sinking again. *He is so perfect in so many ways. If only he weren't such a playboy,* she thought. Taking a swig of her beer, she shook her head to clear the dark thoughts.

"Janet? Did you hear us? We were asking how long Andrew was planning on being in town?"

She forced a professional smile on her face and said, "Probably not much longer. His business here is done."

"Ummm…there's one little piece of business he hasn't finished yet…am I right?" David was looking at her pointedly. "Monkey business with you." Everyone but Janet laughed.

"Yeah, that's not going to happen."

Everyone looked shocked. Radhika was the first to ask, "Why not? You are both so perfect for each other!"

"Not if he's sleeping with his assistant. I don't exactly call that perfect." Janet looked down at the plate of chips in front of her.

All at once, the group burst out in Andrew's defense. "Fiona? No way." "You have to be kidding me." "She's not even pretty!" This last one came from David, who was looking rather agitated.

Radhika had been silent. "Janet. I can tell you with 100 percent certainty that Andrew is not sleeping with Fiona. Winston and I talked about it one night, and he told me that they'd had a fling shortly after you and Andrew broke up, but that was in the past. Janet. Andrew is in love with you."

Elyse confirmed. "She's right. That day when we were building the bunk beds, I overheard him asking Nicole if she knew your ring size and what color diamonds you prefer."

Janet's head started to swirl. *He's not sleeping with Fiona? He's in love with me? He was asking Nicole about a ring?*

It was almost too much to take in.

Coral stood up from the table. "I think it's time we call it a night, ladies. Looks like Janet has a phone call to make."

"I'm glad you called, Red. It feels like forever since we've been alone." Andrew stepped through Janet's front door with one hand behind his back. He presented her with a dozen ruby red roses, wrapped in newspaper. "A peace offering? Even though I'm not really sure what I did. But whatever it was, I'm sorry."

The look in his eyes was so intense that it made her heart stutter in her chest. "How did you get roses this late at night? Everything in town is closed!" Janet pushed her face into the fragrant bouquet and inhaled a deep breath. She was as much trying to calm her heart as she was trying to smell the roses.

"I have friends everywhere," he said, as he took the flowers from her and laid them on the counter. "But there is only one woman I love."

Andrew pulled Janet close, took her by the waist, and pulled her up against his strong, hard body.

"What?" she asked, looking into his eyes.

"I love you, Janet," he said softly. "Even though we've been apart for so long, I knew it the moment I saw you. I realized that I never stopped."

Janet pushed up onto her tiptoes and kissed him. "I never stopped loving you either," she whispered against his mouth. "I'm sorry for the-"

Before she could get the words out, Andrew covered her mouth with a deep kiss.

Janet took his hand and let him through the darkened living room to her bedroom. Before, their need for each other had been insistent, urgent and impatient. But now Andrew was so careful and almost reverent as he pulled her shirt over her head. He leaned in to kiss her again, his mouth hungry and questing as he undid the clasp on her bra, and pulled it off, revealing her breasts. His palms were hot and rough against her nipples. His gentle kneading sent zaps of pleasure to the place between her thighs.

"Andrew," she breathed. "I need you."

"I'm right here, Red. You have me."

He moved them toward the bed, lowering her down gently so that she lay on her back. Janet's fingers fumbled at the drawstring on her linen pants and he helped her pull them off, taking her panties with them.

Andrew leaned back and sighed while gazing down at her. "You're so beautiful," he whispered before covering her mouth with his again.

Janet reached for him, needily grabbing handfuls of his curls and pushing her hand under the t-shirt that she immediately yanked over his head. He caught her wrists, still trapped in the soft fabric, and pinned them over her head. She struggled against him for a moment, but he distracted her by making a trail of kisses from her mouth to her breasts.

When his mouth closed around one of her

nipples, Janet moaned and arched off the bed. No man had been in her bed since they broke up. And Andrew's mouth sucking and nibbling at her sensitive nipples reminded her of why. Andrew was the first, and his hands and mouth reawakened that desire in a way no other man could. She writhed and twisted under his attentions and when his hand finally found its way between her thighs, she cried out.

"Please, Andrew. Please," she begged as his fingertips slipped over her tight bud.

"Shhh…" he quieted as he pulled away and stood at the edge of the bed to take off his pants. He made quick work of it, but her eyes still roamed every beautiful inch of his bared skin. Instead of climbing on top of her, he dropped to his knees and covered her achingly empty core with his mouth. His tongue lathed her clit and her opening with each broad lick and soon she was spiraling toward an intense orgasm.

Her hands, free from his makeshift manacles, grabbed two fistfuls of his hair and pulled him up to meet her. "Inside of me. I want you inside of me when I come."

"Do you have condoms?" he asked.

"No. But there has been no one else…" She hated to break the moment but had to ask. "Do you?"

"No. But I had a complete physical not too long ago. And it's been years for me too. We're good."

Relieved, Janet leaned back on the bed and smiled. "Then, get over here."

Andrew crawled across the bed and settled himself in the cradle of her thighs. She kissed him and tasting herself on his lips made her need spike. She rolled her hips against him until the tip of his cock was positioned at her entrance.

"Please, please, please," she begged again until he finally slid inside of her.

"Oh, god, Red," he murmured against her shoulder as he pressed into her slowly, gently, and carefully.

He moved with slow, shallow thrusts until she began to meet each thrust, seating him deeper. Then he stopped being careful and gentle. He hooked his hand under her knee and pushed her hips wider as he plunged deep, over and over again until she tightened around him, squeezing, triggering a release that made her slipperier and heightened all of the nerve endings inside of her.

"I'm coming..." she moaned but the words had barely left her mouth before it rolled through her, clamping down on his cock so hard that he gritted his teeth and growled.

Before she could catch her breath, he hooked her

knees over his shoulders and pumped into her, hard and fast. Soon she felt the pleasure building again.

"Come with me," he whispered. "I want to feel you coming around me as I come."

His words worked like some kind of spell and with panting breaths and strangled moans Andrew chased her orgasm with his own.

CHAPTER THIRTEEN: THE CALL

For a moment, Andrew was confused. First, there were birds chirping outside. *Why are there birds in my hotel room?* Then, there was an incessant buzzing coming from across the room. *Is that my phone? Why isn't it on the nightstand?* And, last, it appeared from the feel of the sheets on his bare skin that he was naked. *Where are my clothes?*

But before he could open his eyes, the memory came to consciousness. Janet. They made love. Almost all night... The memories stirred in his mind. And soon, something else started to stir.

"Are you going to sleep all day?" Janet walked into her bedroom holding two steaming mugs of coffee.

Sitting up in bed, he answered, "If I can sleep with

you, absolutely." Reaching out for the mug, he heard the buzzing of his phone again.

Janet was looking around for the source of the sound. "Where is it? Under my pants? Your t-shirt? I can't find it!"

Janet looked like a Disney princess the day after a night with her prince. Her red curls fell down over her face as she was bent over looking for his phone. Those delicious breasts were falling out of her robe as she leaned forward, moving pieces of clothes about.

"Leave it, Red. I have something else that's buzzing that needs your attention more…"

"Oh here it is. How did it get under the bed?" Janet handed him the phone, without looking at it.

Reluctantly, Andrew took the phone. "I'll just get rid of whoever it is… Cole? Hey, buddy. Why are you calling so late?" Although it was 9:30 am in Francistown, it was 2:30 in the morning in New York.

"Sorry to call so early. I've been trying to get you all night. It's Ryan. There's been an accident."

Andrew sat up straight in bed. Ryan was Andrew's college friend. Cole and Andrew had been roommates, and across the hall were Ryan and Michael. Ryan was Ryan Cummings, and his family owned Cummings Construction, a large firm in California. Ryan had taken the first few commissions from his role as the lead architect and invested in tech stocks. A couple of good calls meant that he, too, was a billionaire.

Not that any of that mattered now. "How bad is it?"

"We don't know yet. Mike got the call last night and he called me from the plane. I'm headed to London in a couple of hours myself. It doesn't look good, Andrew."

Shit, shit, shit. They were too young to be dealing with this. "I'm on my way."

Janet had been standing nearby, watching, and said, "On your way where? What happened?"

"To London. Ryan has been in an accident."

"Ryan? Ryan Cummings? From college?" Janet looked pale. "Oh my god."

"I have to go." Embracing her, Andrew pleaded, "Will you come with me? Please?"

Janet took a step back. "I can't. I have to stay here. There's Oba and A Place for Grace. And I have meetings with the community leaders. I just can't go."

Pulling on his jeans, and running a hand through his hair to straighten it, he said, "I understand. But I have to go. Ryan, Cole, Mike…we're like brothers. If I can help in any way, I have to be there."

They kissed, and held each other tightly, not

wanting to let go. They had just found each other again. It just wasn't fair. "I'll call you when I land."

As the doors opened to Bart's, St. Bartholomew Hospital in London, Andrew recalled the last time he'd been in a hospital. It was the day his caravan had almost killed Janet. The day he met Oba. The thought of them so far away made his heart sink. But, they had walked out of the hospital with little more than a few scrapes. *Who knows? Maybe Ryan will get lucky, too.*

"Andrew! I'm glad you made it." It was Cole.

"I jumped on the first flight I could catch. I had to fly coach!"

Cole chuckled. "Such indignity! Did you at least have a pretty seatmate?"

"No, it was a very large Irishman named Fergus. Not a good way to spend seven hours, I'll tell you. How's Ryan?"

"Still unconscious. He hasn't woken up since they brought him in two days ago," Cole whispered.

"There he is!" Michael strode toward his two friends and embraced Andrew. "Usually when one of us is passed out for two days, it's you, man." Only a good friend could get away with a comment like that.

"What happened? Why is he in London?"

"Not sure. The last I heard was that Cummings Construction was in talks to build a hotel out here. Kind of a Hotel California vibe. Maybe that's why he was here?" Michael didn't seem to know more than that.

"That's kind of random," Andrew said. "I wonder what the backstory is that led a California construction company to want to build a hotel in London."

Cole chimed in with more information. "Don't know. But they were on their way to tour a potential site when some car came into their lane and crashed head-on. Ryan lost control of the SUV and it rolled. Thank god he was wearing a seatbelt. It saved his life."

Michael added, "They had to cut him out from the car, though. Some kind of head injury. We're not sure."

Andrew looked at his friend, unconscious in a hospital room, far away from his family and felt a rush of emotion. *You have to make it, buddy. We need you. At the very least, I need you in my wedding...*

CHAPTER FOURTEEN: X-RAY VISION

"You hang up first." Janet was laying in bed, Facetiming Andrew. Since London was two hours behind Francistown, it was still dark where he was, but the sun was just coming up through Janet's window.

"I've told you a thousand times, I am not ever going to hang up on you." Andrew's deep voice stirred something primal in Janet.

"A thousand times? Really? Who are you, now? David?" Janet laughed. Andrew had been gone for a little more than three weeks, and they had managed to Facetime every morning since he left.

"How is Ryan's PT coming along?"

Ryan had awakened from his coma a few days after Andrew got to London. He'd had a concussion -

a pretty bad one - and lost some function in his legs. He was doing physical therapy every day to regain his ability to walk normally.

"Pretty good. In fact, I need to get over there early this morning. Mike has to get back to the States, and we are meeting for breakfast before he leaves for Heathrow. What about you? What's my gorgeous girl doing today?"

For all her independence, Janet still swooned when Andrew called her "my girl."

"Just another meeting with the architect on the construction for Extended Grace."

"I love that name, by the way. It's like an African version of Ronald McDonald House, where families can stay together during medical treatment. You have the biggest heart of anyone I've ever met, Red. I love you."

"I love you too, Andrew. I can't wait to see you again."

Pulling on a pair of black slacks and a turquoise top, Janet headed out to kiss Oba in the dining room on her way to her office. *Things are going so well right now*, Janet thought. *A little too well, actually. What do you bet my mother calls today?*

"Mama look! I have a loose tooth!" Oba had just started calling Janet "Mama." At first, Janet felt a little uncomfortable. But Radhika had assured her that Gouta would have wanted her son to call Janet "Mama."

"Why yes, yes you do, little king. It's your first one! When I was a little girl, when I lost a tooth, I put it under my pillow and a fairy left me a dollar for the tooth."

Oba's eyes grew wide. "A fairy! Can I put my tooth under your pillow, too?"

Janet laughed and affectionately patted his head. "We shall see, little king. We shall see."

"I need to see the spreadsheets of the budget forecast for A Place for Grace." Alexis' voice was demanding and shrill as she didn't even bother with saying hello to Janet.

"Good morning to you, too, Mother." *I called it, didn't I?* Janet thought.

"It's not a good morning to me when I am expecting to see a report detailing how the foundation money is being spent and I'm not getting it. What are you doing out there, Janet? Do I need to come out there and see for myself?"

Rolling her eyes, Janet appeased her mother. "No, you don't need to come here. The reason the forecast is late is because I need to see how much we are going to need for Extended Grace. Those figures should be in later today, and I'll have the spreadsheet to you tomorrow."

Just then, there was a knock on Janet's door. "Come in." The door opened to reveal Elyse and Oba standing there. "Mother, I have to go."

Oba was standing with a huge smile on his face and a gap where his front tooth used to be. Extending his hand toward Janet, he proudly stated, "Look, Mama. My tooth is out! Can we put it under your pillow now?"

Walking over to the small boy, she kissed him on the top of the head and took the small pearl of a tooth cradled in his pink palm. "It's supposed to go under YOUR pillow, little king."

Elyse gave her a warning look. How would it look if one of the boys got a visit from the tooth fairy and didn't visit the rest?

"But, you know what? I bet the tooth fairy will think to look under my pillow, too. Let's go put it there for her to find."

"Has he ever had an X-ray of his teeth before?" The dentist was looking at Janet as Oba sat in the huge chair with a paper napkin tied around his little neck.

"No, this is his first time to the dentist. I just

figured since he lost his first tooth this morning, we should have him looked at."

"That's fine. Let's go ahead and get a set of X-rays." Leaning over and whispering to her, the dentist added, "I find that the little ones get nervous. Can you stay with him during the X-rays?" Janet nodded as he handed Oba a lead blanket. "Just put this blanket on your lap."

Handing her a lead vest to wear herself, he asked Janet, "There's no chance you might be pregnant, is there? X-rays can damage a fetus."

Pregnant? Janet started doing mental calculations. Could she be pregnant? Andrew had been gone almost a month. When was her last cycle? Was it before…?

"Little king? Mama is going to step right outside while the nice dentist takes pictures of your teeth. You'll be fine."

Oba was looking at a book of stickers and said, "Okay, mama."

As she closed the door to the exam room, her heart was pounding. Could it be possible?

CHAPTER FIFTEEN: THE BBC

"Are you seriously going to eat all of that?" Cole laughed at Michael, as he sat down at the table in the hospital cafeteria with a heaping plate of scrambled eggs, bacon, sausage, potatoes, beans, tomatoes, fried bread, and for good measure, a slice of dark blood sausage.

"Hey. They don't have a full English fry-up in California. Who knows when I'll get to have this food again?"

Andrew came to the table with a bowl of porridge and steaming hot coffee, nodding at Michael's plate. "Going back to the land of tofu making you hungry? When's your flight, anyway?"

"Actually, it's whenever I want. I booked the jet. The pilot is waiting for me at the airport, in fact."

"Ah, the perks of being a billionaire." To that, all three men toasted with their orange juices and coffees.

Cole commented, "Sadly there are some things money can't buy."

Michael nodded. "I'm just glad Ryan is going to be okay. It was pretty sketchy there for a while."

"Me too," Cole added. Claudia has been bugging me to come home. Gotta keep the woman happy, you know?"

Looking at Andrew, Michael said, "Speaking of which…what's going on with Janet? And where's Winston?"

"Winston actually stayed in Botswana to help make sure that The Department of Mines was going to make good on their promise to the people of Francistown."

"Claudia told me what you did over there. Well done, bro'." Cole playfully punched Andrew on the shoulder. "I wouldn't want to be on your bad side. That's for sure."

"Hahaha. Well. Thanks. It was just the right thing to do. I mean, what's the point of having all this money and power, if we aren't going to use it for good? I just wish I could do more."

Michael agreed. "When my investments took off

and I made all that money, my dad sat me down and talked to me about the responsibility of wealth. He said, 'It's all well and good to have fun, son. But at the end of the day, you're going to be remembered for what you did with your money. Did you make the world a better place, or did you act like that Billionaire Boys' Club, and use your influence the wrong way?' His words always stuck with me."

Cole nodded. "Hey, we're all billionaires. You, me, Andrew, and Ryan in there. We use our money for good. We're The Billionaire Boys' Club 2.0!"

Andrew took a big gulp of his coffee and pushed his chair back. "You know. That gives me an idea. Janet's friend Nicole e-mailed me that the YouTube documentary she did on A Place for Grace is done. Since you guys are heading back Stateside, maybe I can change the perception of the name of the Billionaire Boys' Club. Work with Nicole to bring awareness to the good that billionaires can do. Each one of us has given back in some way. Let's change what people think when they hear the name BBC. Not for ego, of course. But to spread the good word."

The men all stood, and Michael grabbed his laptop bag. "I like it. We can be the BBC 2."

Walking down the hallway to Ryan's room to say goodbye, they were all chuckling. "Leave it to us to come up with a stupid club name after all these years. You can take the boy out of college, but you can't take college out of the boy…"

"A charity gala?" Fiona sounded surprised. "You want me to plan a charity gala? For Janet?"

Fiona had flown back to New York at about the same time Andrew had come to London. They had been working with the time difference for almost a month now, with Fiona handling a lot of the business there.

She'd been asking Andrew when he was going to come home for weeks, but Andrew had been putting her off. If he was going to get on a plane, it was going to be to see Janet.

"No, I'm going to plan the gala. I just need you to handle a few details. And, it's not for Janet. It's for A Place for Grace. We'll have the world premiere of Nicole's documentary, and raise funds for the orphanage, so that innocent children with no family will have a home.."

"Does this mean you aren't coming home? Claudia said that Cole is arriving tomorrow." Fiona was practically whining.

"Is there a problem? If you don't want to do it, I

am sure I can find someone else to…"

"No, no," Fiona interjected. "It's fine. You just caught me off-guard. Email me the list you have so far, and we'll get going."

CHAPTER SIXTEEN: GOODBYES

Janet had one black dress. It was a simple black sheath. Perfect for a funeral.

Gouta had no family, but everyone in the community had loved her. Janet had invited the teachers and staff from the school, and it was likely to be a large, traditional ceremony.

Standing sideways, Janet smoothed the dress down over her belly, peering to see if there were any change. Her abdomen was as flat as ever. *Not for long*, Janet thought.

It had been a few days since the fateful dentist appointment, and Janet's test confirmed the next morning that she was, indeed, pregnant. She was pregnant with Andrew's baby! Although the news had come as quite a shock, Janet was elated. She found herself daydreaming about what the baby would look like. Would he have her red hair? Would she have his piercing eyes?

But Janet hadn't told anyone yet because she wanted Andrew to be the first to know. Their daily Facetime chats had been canceled the last few days - largely because Janet wasn't feeling that well in the mornings anymore.

They would bury Gouta before noon, as was the tradition, so right after breakfast, the small group gathered in the courtyard to get ready to head to the cemetery. Oba looked solemn but strong in his tiny, dark suit. Gouta had been Christian, and the service would be a blend of tribal and Christian expressions.

"Is your man coming?" Elyse asked.

She shook her head but didn't say anything else. She was trying so hard not to let on about the pregnancy that she was afraid to even mention Andrew.

The gravesite was still being dug when they pulled up. Gouta's coffin rested on a wheeled cart under a green tarp. Seats positioned around it in preparation for the service. Oba was at her side, quiet and holding her hand.

"Is Mama in there?" he asked.

"Her body is in there, yes." Janet touched the

centre of Oba's chest and said, "But your mama is in here. Always will be."

She'd been to so many of these, but her tears fell freely. Now that she was about to become a mother herself, she couldn't even imagine the pain of knowing you wouldn't see your child grow up.

Elyse and Coral walked around gathering stones to build a mountain on top of her resting place. Someone started singing and the service got underway.

As the final prayer was being sung, Janet looked over at Oba. His brave face had tears streaming down it. He sat tall in his chair, and he was gripping Janet's hand tightly, his lower lip quivering. He was trying so hard to be brave.

Suddenly, Janet knew. She knew without any reservation that Oba was her son now. That beautiful little boy came into her life for a reason. And that reason was for her to be his mother.

Leaning over to him, she whispered, "I love you, little king."

"I love you too, Mama."

The next day, the phone rang in Janet's office. It was Fiona calling from New York.

"Andrew has been trying to get hold of you." She sounded almost accusatory.

Janet looked at her cellphone and saw four missed calls from Andrew. "I guess I forgot to turn the sound back on after the funeral." Honestly, between the pregnancy fatigue and the emotions from burying a dear friend, all Janet could manage was to tuck Oba into bed and crawl under her own covers.

"Oh yeah. The funeral. Sorry for your loss." She paused long enough to be polite before moving the conversation forward. "Anyway, I guess I'll be the one to tell you. Andrew is planning a charity gala in two weeks to raise money for A Place of Grace."

"Two weeks! How can he plan an entire charity benefit in two weeks?" Janet was both stunned and impressed.

"Andrew has friends in every city, " she said tartly. "Anyway, I'm calling to fill you in on the details. Andrew wants to send the plane and fly you in the day before."

"Wow. I don't know what to say. This is all so sudden."

"Tell me about it." Fiona lowered her voice conspiratorially. "Frankly I was as surprised as you are, given how much he hates kids."

Confused, Janet repeated back, "He hates kids? No, he doesn't. He loves kids."

Fiona chortled. "He loves other people's kids. Sometimes. But we laugh all the time about the poor people who get trapped into having a family. Kind of cramps the billionaire lifestyle, know what I mean?"

Janet leaned back in her chair, in stunned silence. Janet's entire life was built around children. She was adopting Oba. She was PREGNANT! Pregnant by a man who didn't want to have any. What did this mean for them?

After the details of Janet's trip to London were worked out, she hung up the phone in a daze. All she could hear were Fiona's words echoing…"Trapped into having a family. Trapped…"

The last thing she wanted to do was trap Andrew Atherton into anything.

The two weeks had flown by. Janet had talked to Andrew a few times, but he was so busy planning the gala that the conversations had been really short. Which was just fine by Janet. If it were up to her, she wouldn't even go.

However, Nicole had been calling every day, completely excited about her movie premiere.

"I can't wait to see you. This going to be so much fun. We'll have a red carpet, and we've invited

Madonna and Angelina Jolie. They have a soft spot for African orphans, as you can imagine. It's so incredible that Andrew managed to convince them both to come on such short notice!"

Janet didn't really care which celebrities were coming, and she wasn't looking forward to the "fun." She just wanted to get it over with so that she could come home and get on with her life.

Laying in her cold bed alone, the night that Fiona had dropped the bombshell about Andrew's feelings toward having a family, Janet had tossed and turned. As the dawn crept through her window, Janet had come to a conclusion. She wasn't going to tell Andrew about the baby. No, after the gala, Janet was going to break things off with Andrew. This time, the goodbye would be for good.

CHAPTER SEVENTEEN: RELEASED

"Do you have everything?' Andrew carried Ryan's bag containing the few things he'd had brought over to the hospital during the six weeks he stayed there after the accident.

"Yeah, man. I'm good. I can't believe I'm finally getting out of this place. What's been going on in the real world? Did we colonize the moon yet?" Ryan was in good spirits as he was wheeled toward the elevator.

"Not yet, but when we do, I'm sure that your family will be the first to build a hotel there."

"You're funny." Ryan stood and embraced his friend as the driver opened the car door. "Thanks so much for everything, Andrew. I'm still blown away that you all just dropped your lives and came all the way over here for me like that."

Andrew patted his friend on the back. "Hey. We're the BBC 2 now. That's what we do. We're all about charity."

"Ha, the BBC 2. I wonder if that's really going to be a thing now." Sliding into the back seat of the limo, Ryan said, "Are you sure I can't drop you anywhere? Hard Rock? Buckingham Palace? It's the least I can do."

"No, I'm good. I'm actually meeting Winston in Old Bond Street. We have an appointment at Atherton's, London."

"Finally tying the knot, are you two? I always did think you and Winston made a dashing couple..." With that, the door closed and the limo sped off.

"Mr. Atherton. It's an honor to have you here this morning. Here, let me take your coat." Giles Davis wore a stiff grey pinstripe three-piece suit and had a diamond pinky ring on his left hand. "Can I get you something to drink? Coffee, tea, perhaps a breakfast cocktail?" he lowered his voice discreetly.

"No thank you, Gilles. I am waiting on my associate. Bring him back when he arrives." Andrew had spent his life around diamonds and he knew just about everything there was to know about the rare gem. But this wasn't just any old diamond he was buying. This was an engagement ring. For Janet. The first time he'd proposed to her, it was so spur-of-the-moment that they didn't have time to get a ring. Ironic, huh? The heir to a diamond empire proposing without a ring?

Not this time. This time he was going to do it right. On bended knee and the whole thing. Starting with today, and buying the ring.

He surveyed the shiny stones in the glass case. First, he would choose the stone, and then he would choose the setting.

"Sir? Your associate is here."

Winston breezed through the door to the private back room. "Sorry I'm late. The plane was delayed." Winston winked at his old friend.

"You mean *you* were delayed, by Radhika."

"A gentleman never tells," he grinned. "What are we looking at here? Did Nicole ever give you any information on what Janet likes?"

"Nope. Not a word. We are flying blind here, mate."

"Well, do you see anything that catches your eye?"

"Nothing as much as Janet. These are all gorgeous, of course. They're ours. But, I want something a little more…"

"Personal?" Winston added.

"Yes. Something that reflects our history. Something that shows that she is joining our family heritage. WAIT. Winston. You're a genius. I've got it."

Smiling, but a little confused, Winston replied, "If you say so…"

The sun was shining brightly on this crisp London afternoon as Andrew finally stepped out onto Old High Street. Winston and Andrew parted ways, as Andrew had several meetings planned to finalize the details for the gala. There was a lot to do in two days, and Fiona was still in New York. It was up to Andrew to handle the last minute "boots on the ground" details.

As he was walking, enjoying the fresh air, his phone buzzed. He didn't recognize the number, but he answered it anyway.

"Andrew Atherton."

"Andrew. It's Nicole." She sounded breathless.

"Nicole! I didn't recognize your number. How are things going with the documentary?"

"I'm calling from a different phone. My iPhone got stolen!"

"Oh no, I'm sorry." Andrew shook his head.

"That's not even the worst of it. Whoever stole my phone actually hacked into it, and sent a message to everyone in my phone. All of my media contacts. Celebrities. Even my mother."

"I didn't get a message." Andrew looked at his phone. "Oh wait, yes I did. Since it's a hacker, I'm not going to open it. What did it say?"

"The theft wasn't random, Andrew. The person who stole my phone said that they are going to release a YouTube video at the same time as the premiere."

"So, what does it have to do with us? YouTube is a huge platform. What do we care about some other documentary?"

"The video is about you."

"Me? What about me?" Andrew was confused.

"It's an exposé on you and your friends. The Billionaire Boys' Club Two."

"What? No. No one can have anything bad on any of us. This has to be some kind of hoax."

"It's not. Come to my office and I'll show you the video. Andrew, this could ruin the gala. And my career!"

Standing behind Nicole, looking over her shoulder at the computer monitor, Andrew was sickened at what he was seeing. It was dark video footage of himself and Mykel Batou that night at the cemetery. Andrew's hands were at Mykel's throat and it looked like he was assaulting a government official.

"Who took this?" Andrew demanded.

"I don't know. It could be anyone. Everyone has cell phones these days."

"Well, this isn't enough to make a movie with. It's just a clip."

"Watch this." Nicole fast-forwarded to the next video clip.

"Is that Ryan's accident?" Andrew saw a black SUV flipping and crashing.

"Yes. The narrator said that he was driving recklessly."

"He was swerving to avoid the other car! This is crazy."

"There's more, Andrew. The whole movie is clips of the four of you, taken out of context. It's pieced together to make you guys all look like rich, spoiled brats who pretend to do philanthropy but really just use it as an excuse to do whatever you want."

Andrew slumped down in the chair next to Nicole's desk. He didn't even notice the expansive view of London out of her top, corner office window. This would taint A Place for Grace. If it got out. "What do they want? What can we do to stop the release?"

"I don't know yet. I'll let you know when I hear from whoever is doing this." Nicole put her head in her hands. "I'm meeting Janet at the airport tomorrow and we're going to do some shopping after she gets settled at the Ritz...I don't know if she knows anything, but I don't want to be the one to tell her that her charity gala is in jeopardy."

"Don't. Don't say a word. I'll handle this. I'll find a way to stop this piece of shit from being released."

CHAPTER EIGHTEEN: CITY LIGHTS

Looking out the window of the private jet, Janet tried to remember the last time she had been in a city as large as London. She'd been living in Botswana for several years now, and the simpler life had become the norm.

Yet, here she was, on a Gulfstream IV, indulging in Godiva chocolates and non-alcoholic apple cider. The flight attendant had offered champagne but fortunately didn't ask any questions when Janet turned it down.

"You better enjoy it while you can, little princess. This is the last time we'll be enjoying your daddy's money."

Janet didn't know if the baby was a girl, of course.

It was too soon. But she secretly hoped to have a daughter with dark black curls, like Andrew.

Tears threatened to sting her eyes, and so she forced herself to think of other things. "It will be great to see your Aunt Nicole again," Janet told the baby. "Even if I can't tell her about you."

It was strange to not have a cellphone with her on a trip like this. But they didn't exactly have an Apple Store in Francistown, and her phone wasn't working after Oba accidentally dropped it in a puddle. "I'm sorry, Mama. I was trying to take a picture of the tadpoles." She was hoping Nicole would take her to one in London so she could be connected to the world again.

Fortunately, the flight went quickly, as there were several in-flight videos to choose from. The excitement of the trip, plus the fatigue that comes from growing a baby helped Janet to drift off to sleep.

"Miss. Miss? We are about to land."

Janet had been dreaming of Andrew. Again. It seemed that every night she dreamed of them in some romantic destination. Paris. Rome. The Empire State Building. In the dream, they were always kissing, as a gentle rain fell down on them, by the light of a full moon.

"Maybe these are experiences you will have, little princess. Maybe my dreams are for you."

"Private jets definitely agree with you! You're positively glowing!" Nicole rushed to hug her friend.

"You're too kind. I'm not nearly as glamorous as you are, my dear. But I am starving. Where can we get a big, juicy hamburger?"

"Ha! It's 9:00 am!"

"That's lunchtime at home. Get me some fries in my belly!" The women linked arms and laughed as they walked to Nicole's Jaguar.

After stuffing their faces at The Diner Soho, they headed out for an afternoon of shopping. "I need to get a new phone. Oba dropped mine in a puddle and it hasn't worked for days."

Nicole made a strange face at that, and said, "Oh! I was wondering why I hadn't gotten any calls from you. But I figured it was because my phone was stolen."

"Your phone was stolen? Well, then let's both stop by the Apple Store."

Nicole hesitated. "Uh, well. Maybe later. We have a lot to do before the gala tomorrow."

"Okay, just so long as I get one before I go back to Botswana. The one in Gaborone is too far out of the way."

Four hours later, and laden with shopping bags, Janet was exhausted. She and Nicole had hit almost every high-end boutique in London. Plus, she'd had her hair cut, they'd gotten facials, and manicures. The last stop was to get some new earrings to compliment her gown.

Frankly, Janet didn't want to shop anymore. The idea of a warm bath and a comfortable bed was calling to her. But Nicole's pleading won her over.

"Please. Atherton London is right here. Then I'll take you to your hotel. I promise."

Walking in the doors, and seeing diamonds everywhere, Janet's heart went to her throat. The first time Andrew had proposed, he'd said he would bring her to his company's New York store to get her engagement ring. But one thing led to another, and it never happened.

Placing her hand protectively over her belly, Janet thought, *And now it never will happen.*

Fortunately, The Ritz London was only a five-minute drive from Atherton London. "You sure you don't want me to help you up with your things?" Nicole had pulled her black Jag up to the valet. "I don't mind…"

"No, I'm fine. The porter can get my bags." It hadn't been so long that Janet forgot what it was like to stay at an expensive hotel. After all, she was raised a Girard.

"Alright, then. I'll see you tomorrow at the gala!" Janet watched as Nicole sped off.

"We have you in the Penthouse Suite, Ms. Girard. Mick here will bring up your things. Will there be anyone joining you that might need a key?" The man at the front desk lowered his voice slightly as he said the last part.

"No, it's just me."

Janet had to admit it felt very strange to be in such a luxurious setting after living in a cottage at an orphanage for so long.

Waiting for the elevator to take her to the penthouse, Janet could smell something delicious coming from Berners Tavern. The scent caused her stomach to growl and she realized that she was hungry again. "Little princess, I might have to rename you large queen. You've given me quite an appetite!"

Janet's room was breathtaking. She never would have chosen the Penthouse Suite for herself. It was bigger than her cottage! She wasn't sure which to do first, sit out on one of the three outdoor terraces and take in the London view, or strip off her traveling clothes and stand under the rainforest shower.

What Janet really wanted to do was check her

messages. Without a phone for two days, she had no idea what was going on with Andrew. Plus, she wanted to call Oba and say goodnight. But, they hadn't gotten to the Apple Store today, so she would have to use the phone in her room. Expensive, yes. But what about this weekend wasn't?

Opening the fridge in the kitchen, Janet marveled at the selection of treats. She chose a sparkling water and went to go explore the rest of the suite.

In the master bedroom, on top of the plush king-sized bed, was a small envelope. Picking it up, she recognized the handwriting and her name on the outside. Inside, was a card that simply said, "You are my beloved. Andrew."

Tossing herself onto the bed, Janet began to cry. "It's not fair, little princess. But you deserve to be wanted and loved. And I will give you that life if it's the last thing I do." The tears subsided only as Janet drifted off to sleep, with the city lights of London reflecting in the mirror.

CHAPTER NINETEEN: COLLATERAL DAMAGE

Andrew was feeling a little better. He was in the middle of his five-mile run on the Ritz Carlton's treadmill and he was thinking about Janet. Just knowing that he was on the same property as Janet made him feel closer to her. But, he wanted to wait until the gala to see her. He didn't want to risk her finding out anything about the exposé. Or the engagement ring. She always did have a way of getting secrets out of him…and they had a lifetime to share together. Just one more day, and then Janet Girard would be his fiancée again.

He knew he was taking a bit of a risk booking her in the Penthouse Suite, just a few doors down from his own seventh-floor loft. But he wanted only the best for her from now on.

The treadmill beeped that his workout was over. Taking a swig from his water bottle, Andrew checked his phone for messages. There was one from Winston, another from Fiona, but nothing from Nicole about the video.

Wiping the sweat from his brow, the phone in his hand started to ring. It was Claudia.

"Hey, sis'."

"How's my favorite employee?" Claudia loved to tease her brother.

"Hard at work. I deserve a raise, don't you think?"

"Very funny. The check is in the mail. How's everything coming along for the gala tonight? I'm sorry I can't be there. We have way too much going on here in New York to get away."

"No worries, sis. This isn't an official Atherton Diamonds event anyway. Things are looking good. Fiona got into town yesterday, and we're meeting this morning to go over the timeline."

Andrew hadn't mentioned anything to Claudia or Cole about the exposé. Since she and Nicole weren't really friends, the hacker hadn't sent them the message about the video. Andrew also hadn't mentioned the proposal. Better to keep everything quiet so there was less chance of Janet finding out.

At least Claudia's attitude toward Janet had

changed. His heart warmed to think of her. Janet had a captivating effect on everyone - his sister included.

"I'm about to get into the elevator. I'll call you tomorrow."

"Okay, so the celebrities are going to start walking up the red carpet at 6:00." Fiona and Andrew sat at a nearby Starbucks. While Fiona was pointing to the timeline, Andrew kept looking at the door every time it opened.

"Hello? Earth to Andrew. Are you even listening?"

"Oh, yeah. I'm sorry."

"Are you waiting for someone? Or avoiding someone?" Fiona leaned in close to Andrew. "Did you and Janet have a fight?"

Still looking at the door, he shook his head. "No. No fight. I just don't want to run into anyone this morning. Too much to do."

"Exactly, which is why we need to go over this timeline. So, red carpet at 6:00. The photographers will get there at 5:30. I think you and I should get there about halfway through the red carpet event. We don't want to be first, but we don't want to be so late that the photographers have left."

"Wait… we?"

"Yes. We. You and me."

"Why would I be walking the red carpet with you? Aren't you bringing a date?"

"Andrew. Why would I bring a date? This is a work event. For both of us. I just assumed we would be going together. We always go to these kinds of events together."

"Fiona this is different. Tonight is about Janet. I'm bringing her. She is the star tonight. It's her efforts that have saved so many children from homelessness. She's the one who founded A Place for Grace. This isn't just some business function. I thought you understood."

For a moment, Fiona looked crestfallen. But, she regained her composure and said, "Got it, Boss. I'll ride with Winston and Radhika. Okay, so after the red carpet is the champagne reception, sponsored by Dom Perignon…"

They'd spent about an hour going over the final details of the gala before Fiona left to go get ready. Andrew never understood why it took women so long to get ready for these things. Especially when they were naturally beautiful, like Janet. *I guess some women just need more work than others*, he thought.

Reaching down to get his laptop bag, Andrew saw something on the floor under the seat where Fiona had been sitting. Reaching down to grab it, he saw that it was a flash drive. Fiona must have dropped it when she pulled her notebook out of her bag.

It wasn't like him to snoop, but he also needed to check if the flash drive belonged to Atherton. It could contain sensitive company information, so just to be safe, Andrew pulled out his MacBook and plugged the drive in.

As it was loading, Andrew's phone rang. "Mike. I'm glad you called back. I need a favor."

Andrew detailed what was going on. Nicole's phone getting stolen and hacked. The message that went out to her entire contact list. The video that made all four of the men look like spoiled rich jerks instead of philanthropists.

"What did they think they have on me?" Michael was concerned. He didn't want his parents to see some movie filled with lies about him.

"I couldn't stomach watching the whole thing. After they tried to make Ryan's accident look like reckless driving, I turned it off. But the message said that the video would be posted on YouTube at the same time our documentary was going to premiere. So, that's 8:00."

"How can I help?"

"Well, since 8:00 in London is noon in California,

what I need from you will be in the middle of the day tomorrow for you."

"Not a problem. What do you need?"

"Are your parents still couple friends with Susan Wojcicki and her husband?"

"The head of YouTube? Yeah. We saw them at Christmas last year." Michael's parents were early investors in Google, and Michael even did an internship there one summer when they were in college. He'd known Susan and Dennis practically his whole life.

"Can you make a few calls for me?"

"If it means that my parents won't see that video, I'm in."

Setting the phone down, Andrew grabbed another cup of coffee and opened the file on the flash drive. As the images popped up on the screen, Andrew couldn't believe what he was seeing. The drive did belong to Fiona. And, along with all of the spreadsheets and company information was a video file. It was simply called YouTube.

No. It can't be…

Andrew clicked on the video, and it began to play. The narrator's voice was female, but it was altered with a voice changer so he couldn't recognize it. "What you are about to see is the REAL story behind

The BBC 2. These four college friends, Andrew Atherton, Cole Bennett, Ryan Cummings, and Michael Davis, are all billionaires. Their image is that of philanthropy…but the real story is one of rich men who think they are above the law…"

Why would Fiona have that video on her flash drive? There was only one explanation. She was the only person to have access to the footage. She was in Botswana when Andrew had his confrontation. He'd sent her footage of Ryan's car accident. She worked with Claudia to get Cole to invest in the mine. Lord only knows what she twisted around to use against him - and Mike. She must have arranged for someone to steal Nicole's phone, too.

There was only one reason he could think of that Fiona would do such a thing. To hurt Janet by discrediting him. Janet was Fiona's target, and Andrew and the rest of the BBC 2 were just collateral damage.

Andrew felt sick. Slamming his full coffee into the trash, he grabbed his computer and stormed out of Starbucks. Whatever Fiona thought she was going to do, she had another thing coming.

CHAPTER TWENTY: RED ON THE CARPET

Janet took one last look at her reflection in the mirror before heading downstairs. "Little princess, I think your Aunt Nicole is right. Being pregnant with you does agree with me."

She was wearing a floor-length silver satin evening gown. The bias cut clung to her curves, and the plunging neckline hugged her growing breasts. Janet could see a slight curve in her belly where a baby bump was beginning to emerge. But, if you didn't know about the pregnancy, it just looked like a pretty rounded belly.

Janet's red hair was pulled back into an elegant side ponytail, and her new emerald earrings sparkled, drawing attention to her long neck. Cherry red lipstick adorned her full lips, and a light touch of eye makeup complemented the look.

Twirling in the mirror, Janet loved the way the dress moved with her. *Oh, little princess. I hope you are a girl and get to feel this way. Even just for one night.*

Slipping on the clear high heels, Janet grabbed her bag and looked around for her phone before remembering she didn't have one and headed downstairs.

The classical music in the elevator didn't have its intended effect of being soothing. Janet's stomach was in knots. She hadn't seen Andrew in more than a month. So much had happened since that night of passion. She couldn't let herself think that this would be the last night they would be together…

As the elevator doors opened and Janet crossed the lobby, heels clicking on the marble floors, she could feel the heads turning to stare at her.

Janet did feel like a celebrity tonight. London was a far cry from Francistown. And while she missed Oba terribly, she was determined to enjoy this night.

Suddenly, on the other side of the glass doors, she saw him. He was looking down at his phone and hadn't seen her yet. *My god, he is beautiful.*

Wearing a black tuxedo, the form-fitting shirt clung to that chest. Janet's heart pounded remembering every inch of his body. The tailored pants highlighted his long legs. The jacket strained at his broad shoulders. But the thing that got her the most was that hair. Those curls that were perfect for grabbing in the heat of passion.

Stop. Don't think that, Janet. Don't remember those things. Just focus on the gala.

Andrew stood outside the doors of the Ritz Carlton. Although it was a little silly to stand outside the hotel he'd been living at for the last several weeks, he felt it was necessary. Just a few more hours and he could tell Janet everything.

Before he saw her, his phone dinged. It was Mike. One simple text message. "Called Susan. She was pissed. She's on board. As soon as the video is posted, Susan will pull it.."

Andrew smiled. Looks like he isn't the only ones with friends in high places.

Looking up, through the glass doors, Andrew saw her. For a moment, he thought he was dreaming. *That can't be her. She looks like a movie star.*

Their eyes met. The glass doors of the hotel opened, and Janet approached Andrew. Time stopped for a moment as they just gazed at each other. Neither one wanted to break the spell.

"Excuse me. Miss?" A little girl with dark curly hair and piercing blue eyes was standing next to them, looking at Janet.

"Yes, sweetheart?" Janet bent down to the girl's eye level.

"Are you a princess?" The little girl looked away shyly.

Andrew answered her. "Yes, young lady. She is."

The flashing lights of the cameras sounded like popcorn as Janet stepped out of the limo. "Ms. Girard! Over here!" Andrew's arm felt steady and strong as Janet fought to savor the moment. It was a little overwhelming!

The gala was being held at the Andaz London, one of the most popular spots for movie premiers. The hotel had been built at the turn of the century and was finished in 1901. But it wasn't until the late 1990s that a secret space was discovered behind a fake wall. It had been built in 1912 and was a grand, opulent room made with twelve different kinds of Italian marble on the floor, walls and columns, mahogany panels, an organ, candelabras and a blue and gold domed ceiling decorated with zodiac signs. It was unlike anything Janet had ever seen in her life.

Walking over to the bar area, they saw that Winston and Radhika were already there. As soon as Radhika saw Janet, she practically sprinted over to her.

"Janet! Can you believe this place? A far cry from the lobby at the Department of Mines, isn't it?"

Janet embraced her friend. "It's magnificent."

"Look. Over there. Angelina Jolie is here with all of her kids. They are talking with Oprah and Stedman. I can't believe I am here."

Janet was glad for her friend that she was able to share in this glamorous event.

"Can I get you a drink?" Andrew asked as he leaned down to Janet's ear.

Radhika interjected before Janet could answer. "Actually, I want to steal her away to the little girl's room first."

"Sounds good. I have to go check on some things, anyway. Meet you back here in a few."

As Radhika and Janet made their way across the crowded room, she whispered into Janet's ear, "Does Andrew know yet?"

Janet stopped and looked at her friend. "Know what?"

"About the baby."

"Wait, how did you..."

Radhika just smiled and kept walking. "That glow on your skin isn't just from love, my friend."

CHAPTER TWENTY ONE: GRACEFUL EXIT

"How are we doing?" Andrew looked at the clock on the wall and it said 7:05. He was in a back office of the Andaz, with a security team of people and a bank of computers monitoring YouTube.

"Nothing yet, boss. Looks like he's waiting until 8 as promised."

Or SHE is, Andrew thought bitterly.

"Sounds good. Keep me posted. I need to get back down there so no one gets suspicious."

Slipping out the door, Andrew ran into Nicole in the hallway. She looked beautiful in a floor-length black gown, but Andrew didn't even notice. His mind was on getting back to Janet.

"What's going on? Are we still okay?" Nicole looked worried.

"We're good. Mike is at the YouTube headquarters in California right now, with the head of the company. She is couple friends with his parents."

"Wow."

"Anyway, as soon as the video posts, Susan is going to pull it."

"Why do we need all these guys on this end, then?"

"Because I'm not about to take a chance on our reputation. Mistakes happen. I don't want ANYONE seeing that video. It would ruin lives. It would ruin Janet's reputation if investors - and her mother - thought that someone disreputable had donated the land. I won't risk it. If for some reason, the video plays, the security team here will kill the Internet at the hotel. That would buy us time to get it pulled in California."

"I, for one, am glad. Let's head back down before anyone notices that we're missing."

Dinner had already started when Nicole and Andrew walked up to their table.

"Where have you two been?" Ryan was seated

opposite from Winston and Radhika, and there were two empty spaces in between him and Janet.

"Oh, just attending to last-minute gala stuff," Andrew said as he pulled out Nicole's chair, seating him next to Ryan. "Have you two met?"

"No, I haven't had the pleasure." Ryan tried to stand and shake Nicole's hand, but he winced in pain and had to sit back down. "I'm Ryan. The brains behind the BBC 2."

Nicole laughed as she sat down next to him. "I see. The brains, huh? Then what is Andrew?"

"Andrew? Oh, he's the brawn. If we ever need heavy stuff lifted, or someone to sprint really fast across a parking lot, he's the one we call."

They were both chuckling. Nicole extended her hand, and said, "Well, I'm Nicole. It's nice to meet you, Ryan. I'm neither the brains nor the brawn around here…"

Ryan quipped, "Well, then you must be the beauty."

Nicole blushed as she leaned over and said softly, "I was really sorry to hear about your accident. You're really fortunate to have such loyal and amazing friends. It speaks well of your character."

Just then, a woman came up to Nicole and whispered in her ear. Nicole stood up, and said to the group, "If you'll excuse me, it's almost time to premiere the documentary, "Amazing Grace."

~

Radhika leaned across the table and whispered to Janet. "Where's Fiona? I haven't seen her tonight."

Janet realized that she hadn't either. She was about to ask Andrew when she heard his name being announced on stage.

"And now, ladies and gentlemen," Nicole said to the well-dressed crowd, "let's have a round of applause for the man who has made this night possible. Andrew Atherton."

He stood and made his way up to the stage. Standing in front of a large movie screen, he looked poised as he spoke to the crowd.

"A few months ago, I was in Botswana on a business deal, when I met a group of people who would change my life."

The crowd gave Andrew their rapt attention, as he continued. " It's been almost thirty-five years since the Live Aid concert that benefited the people of Africa. And, while massive strides have been made, there is still a crisis there. The AIDS epidemic has affected, probably, every person in this room in one way or another. But we are the lucky few. The chosen ones, if you will, with the resources to afford this thousand-dollars-a-plate dinner. Right now, in another part of the world, there are hundreds of families who can't afford basic medical treatment. Families whose loved ones are dying, leaving children orphaned. But there is a group of people - tireless workers - dedicated to helping ease the crisis. And, tonight, I want to introduce you to one of them. Ladies and Gentlemen, I want to introduce the woman who is the real reason we are here tonight. Ms. Janet Girard."

Andrew stepped down from the stage and gave Janet a polite kiss as she made her way past him. He wanted more, but not with a thousand watching eyes from the audience.

The bright lights blinded Janet as she took the mic. "Thank you so much, Andrew, for the kind words. But I'm not the real reason we are here tonight. The real reason we are here is because of the kids. And my dear friend Nicole was kind enough to create this documentary that shows what my organization, A Place of Grace, is all about. I know we're all excited to see the movie, but let me just take a couple of minutes to give you the backstory of how A Place of Grace came to be."

As Andrew headed back to the table, he placed another sealed note on Janet's chair. He then patted Winston on the back, and made a graceful exit out a side door, unnoticed by Janet. He heard the sound of applause as he headed back up to the offices.

CHAPTER TWENTY TWO: DROPPED

Andrew made his way down the hallway to the back offices of the Andaz Hotel. Behind him, he could hear the laughter and applause of the audience as Janet and Nicole were hosting the gala. A quick glance at his watch told him he'd better hurry. It was almost 8:00.

Turning around a corner in the brightly lit hallway, Andrew literally crashed into someone going the opposite way.

"Andrew! I didn't expect to see you here...why aren't you out at the gala?" It was Fiona.

Seething, Andrew put on his best poker face and smiled. "Fiona! I was looking for you! No one had seen you at the gala, and we wondered where you might be. I opened this door, and it led me down this hallway. What a coincidence that you're here. Let me just text the others and let them know I found you."

Looking down at his phone and texting, Andrew thought, *I should have been an actor. Looks like she bought it.* The text was really to Winston. "Call the police. Have them meet me in the back office at the Andaz."

"I think we need to go this way," Andrew said, as he took Fiona's arm and led her toward the offices. Glancing at his watch again, he picked up the pace a little. It was 7:54 pm.

"Who are you texting, Winston?" Radhika whispered. "The movie is about to start."

"I'll explain later," he whispered back. It was six minutes until the movie was to be released on YouTube, and six minutes until every person in this room would receive an email, text, or push notification that the expose telling the "real story" had been dropped at the same time. Reputations and careers were on the line.

Winston kissed Radhika on the cheek as he stepped out of the room for a moment to call the police. From the other room, he heard Nicole on stage, talking.

"So when Janet invited me to A Place for Grace to volunteer, of course I said yes. What you are about to see is the footage from that day. It captures the life and feel of the orphanage. The heartbreaking story of a little boy who was losing his mother. And the courageous woman who fought to build a home for the hundreds of children displaced…"

As Nicole was introducing the film, Janet ducked her head and headed back to her seat at the table. Instantly, she noticed that Andrew was not there. Where was he? The movie is about to start.

It was then that she saw the note at her seat. It was the same size and handwriting as the one that was on her bed. *Andrew.*

Quietly tearing open the envelope, she held the notecard below the edge of the table so that no one could see that she was reading. The note said:

Something has come up and I need to go. Meet me at the base of the London Eye at midnight. We need to talk.

Janet's heart sunk. Did he know about the baby? Is that why he left? She knew that she had planned to end things with him tonight, anyway. But, she'd hoped that they would have at least one evening together before it happened.

Oh well, little princess. Fairy tales don't always come true, do they?

Janet's thoughts were interrupted by Nicole's voice from the stage. "And now, the moment we have all been waiting for. I present to you, Straw Barn Publishing's first-ever documentary, "Amazing Grace."

The crowd applauded. The lights dimmed. The screen lit up.

It was go-time. 7:59 pm. Andrew had Fiona by the arm as he was hustling down the hall to the office. He wanted her to see that her plan wasn't going to work. And he wanted to see her face when she realized it.

"Andrew! You're hurting my arm! Why are we walking so fast? I think this is the wrong direction!" Fiona was struggling to keep up with Andrew's pace.

"No, Fiona. This is exactly right where you need to be."

Andrew opened the doors to the office and could see YouTube up on several screens.

"Hey, boss. Nothing yet. We have several channels on screen, from a bunch of different influencers. If something goes wrong, this is gonna drop worldwide. In about sixty seconds."

Fiona looked completely confused. "Where are we? Who are these people?" She turned to Andrew and demanded, "What is going on?"

Finally, Andrew let his anger show. "Why don't you tell me?"

"I don't know what you mean?" Fiona looked at him innocently.

"Don't bullshit me. You have been planning this behind my back for weeks. You got footage from A Place for Grace, footage of me at the cemetery, images of Ryan's accident..." He was getting so mad that he was afraid he might lose it.

Taking a deep breath, he calmed and continued. "You sent that stuff to a producer and had a video made. You had Nicole's phone stolen, and then had a hacker send a message to everyone in her contact list. And you did ALL of it, while looking me straight in the eye and pretending to be a loyal employee."

Fiona just looked down at the ground. Tears filled her eyes as she looked up at him.

"Do you know why I did it, Andrew? Do you know why?"

"No, and I don't care."

"I did it because I love you. I have always loved you. From the time we were together until now, I knew that I was the right one for you. But, you had to go and run into Janet again. Fall in love with her. I knew that if I could get her out of the picture, you'd come back to me."

"That makes no sense. You hurt me and my friends so that I would fall in love with you?" Andrew stared at Fiona in disbelief. "Are you really that demented?"

Bitterness swept across Fiona's face. "You don't get it, do you? You and your friends are BILLIONAIRES. You have everything. You always land on your feet. My stupid documentary might dent your image for a few weeks. But, you'll always still be rich. You'll always still have the power to get what you want. That's what money does."

"Guys. Look." One of the security team pointed to the computer monitor. Music began to play, and some video footage from a drone started. "What you are about to see is the REAL story behind The BBC 2. These four college friends, Andrew Atherton, Cole Bennett, Ryan Cummings, and Michael Davis, are all billionaires. Their image is that of philanthropy… but the real story is one of rich men who think they are above the law…"

∽

Janet wished that Andrew were here to see this. The documentary was magnificent. Images of Andrew and Oba, working together to build the bunk beds. Wide, expansive scenes of A Place for Grace. Elyse in her office. Radhika and Winston, laughing. Coral having a pillow fight with one of the kids. Even Janet, in her cottage. Although it was strange to see herself up on a movie screen, she knew it was for a good cause. But, it really did make her miss home...

I'll be home soon, little king, Janet thought. *And we can start our life as a family...*

Looking around the room, everyone else seemed to be riveted to the screen. Janet could see Angelina and her kids, Oprah and Stedman, and on the other side, Madonna and her kids, with an entourage of admirers. The room was filled with government officials, dignitaries, celebrities, humanitarians, and other people of influence. Five hundred people who could all make a difference in the lives of the African people. Not to mention five hundred people who paid one thousand dollars a plate to be here. That money meant that Janet wouldn't need the Girard Foundation money for a very long time.

How had Andrew managed to pull this off in two

weeks? And, where was he? He should be here to see the fruits of his labor.

Andrew sent Winston a text. "What's going on? Are people's phones going off?" Andrew could imagine five hundred phones buzzing and beeping at the same time, as the hacker sent out an alert that the exposé had dropped. While not everyone would stop and watch it right then, enough of them would. *Even if one person does, it will spread like wildfire...*

The security room was silent as the images on the screen continued. Were Mike and Susan going to pull the video in time? Onscreen, Andrew saw his face, and photos of Michael, Ryan, and Cole. Closed captioning had their names right there, in print.

Andrew looked at Fiona, who was watching the monitors with a smug grin.

Come on, Mike. This is going to destroy us.

All at once, the room let out a sigh of relief. The images of the movie were replaced with a black screen that said, "This video is no longer available on YouTube."

Fiona became indignant. "Wait? What? How did

you..." Just then, the doors burst open. "Fiona Durant. You are under arrest."

"On what charges?" she demanded. "It's not illegal to release a YouTube video?"

"No, but defamation of character is. And slander, libel, and arranging for theft and phone hacking."

"But the video was pulled before it aired."

"Enough of it ran, and we have evidence that at least a few people saw it. I'd get yourself a good barrister, Ms. Durant. Now, please, come with us."

Fiona turned and glared at Andrew as she was being escorted out the door. "See what I mean? You rich folks always land on your feet."

Andrew just smiled at her and said, "Fiona. You're fired."

CHAPTER TWENTY THREE: THE EYES HAVE IT

The line of cars outside the Andaz was impressive - not only for how many cars there were, but for the opulence. Rolls Royces jockeyed for position with Porsches, Lamborghinis, Maseratis, and of course hundreds of limos. There were headlights and tail lights as far as the eye could see. A light mist was falling, and everything glistened in the light of the full moon.

It would have been a perfect night for romance, except...

Janet stood next to Nicole, Winston, and Radhika watching as the crowd trickled out into the street, looking for their cars and drivers. They could overhear comments about the evening, as the guests passed by.

"I was crying at the end! It was so beautiful."

"I just hope I can make a difference in the world like that."

"That little boy Oba is so cute. I want him!"

"That Andrew Atherton is sure easy on the eyes…"

Andrew. Somehow Janet needed to get to the London Eye by midnight. It was less than three miles away, but with this traffic, she had no idea how she would ever make it.

"Miss Girard?" Janet turned to see a man wearing a chauffeur's uniform standing behind her.

"Yes?"

"Mr. Atherton asked that you come this way."

The others in her small group had overheard, and all smiled, hugging her goodbye. "Have fun!" "You deserve it!"

But Radhika leaned over, and as she kissed Janet's cheek, whispered. "Listen to the man. Listen to what he tells you. Look in his eyes and you will see the truth."

Janet nodded weakly. *I already know the truth. I have to tell him goodbye.*

Winding down a maze of brightly-lit hallways and

what appeared to be secret doors, Janet was sure they were going the wrong way.

"Just a few more minutes, Madam. I assure you. This is the fastest route."

"Where are we going?"

"This door will take us to Alderman's Walk. It's a passageway that leads to the large house and gardens of Sir Francis Dashwood."

"I have somewhere to be. I need to get to..."

"I know, Madam. Just trust me. You'll see."

A few minutes later, Janet was surprised to see a sleek black helicopter waiting on the lawn. "A helicopter? You expect me to get into that?"

"Mr. Atherton sent it for you. It's the fastest transportation at the moment."

Unsure, as she ducked her head under the spinning blades of the copter, she got inside. It was deafeningly loud. The pilot handed her some headphones and shouted, "Here, put these on."

As Janet placed them over her cold ears, the helicopter started to rise. She could see the London Wall below her, as the body of the copter tipped and flew off. The city lights of London floated below her like fireflies. The River Thames glittered under the full moon.

Janet's stomach started fluttering. *Is that you, little*

princess? I can't wait to show you the world...

Coming into view was the London Eye. Currently, Europe's tallest Ferris Wheel. It was incredible to think that it was below her. And even more incredible to think that Andrew was down there, somewhere, waiting for her.

Touchdown was much smoother than in an airplane. It was more like a bird landing on a branch. Taking the headphones off, Janet thanked the pilot and was helped out of the helicopter.

Sure glad I'm wearing a gown and high heels, she thought sarcastically. *It's a great night for a hike.*

Looking around, slightly disoriented, Janet didn't see him at first. But the din of the helicopter quieted as it sped away, and Janet heard her name.

"Janet. I'm here."

Walking toward her was the man she loved. The man whose baby she carried. And the man she needed to leave. It was almost too much to bear.

Pushing the thoughts out of her mind for a moment, Janet chattered about the documentary. She told him how the audience loved it, and how everyone laughed when Oba said he wanted to grow up to be a "dock worker" instead of a doctor.

All the while, Andrew was quiet. Janet suspected that he'd found out about the baby somehow and was going to tell her it was over. She needed to break it off with him first.

"Andrew, look. There is something I need to tell you…"

"Janet. Please. Let me go first."

They were standing in front of the London Eye. It was lit up, but there was no one on it. Andrew opened the door to one of the passenger capsules, and said, "Here. Let's talk in here."

"This night has sure had a lot of ups and downs already," Janet quipped. "What's one more?" Secretly, she was glad to get inside and out of the cold. *Satin isn't exactly the warmest fabric.*

As the Ferris Wheel began to move, Janet got another perspective. What had seemed so far away in the helicopter was so much closer now.

As they reached the apex of the wheel, the movement stopped. It was just like one of Janet's dreams. A full moon…a gentle rain…

"Janet, I have loved you since the day we met. As you know, I was a complete workaholic. But you inspired me to see the world. You've inspired me to be a better person. Because of you, I want to make the world a better place. YOU did that. You are the most amazing, generous, compassionate woman I have ever met."

Andrew stood, pulled something out of his pocket, and got down on one knee in front of Janet. "Janet Girard. I would be the luckiest man on the planet if you would agree to be my wife."

Janet was stunned. Before her was the most magnificent diamond ring she had ever seen. Its sparkle beckoned her in the light of the moon.

"It was my grandmother's. Five carats. She wore it for sixty years. Claudia sent it to me this week when I told her I was going to ask you to marry me. She even hired a bodyguard to fly over with it to make sure it got here safely."

Janet wanted nothing more than to wear that ring for another sixty years. But, with tears in her eyes, she looked at her beloved, and simply said, "No."

Time stopped for a moment as the look on Andrew's face morphed from one of love to one of confusion. "No?"

"Andrew. I can't."

Shaking his head a little to make sure he was hearing correctly, Andrew repeated, "You can't? Why not?"

Janet had promised herself that she wasn't going to say anything. She planned to simply say that she didn't love him and that she wanted to end things.

But her mouth couldn't form the lies. Instead, it all came rushing out, in tears.

"Andrew. I'm pregnant. I'm pregnant and I don't want to burden you. I don't want to be one of those people you and Fiona laugh at…"

"Fiona!" Andrew stood up. "What did she tell you?"

Sobbing now, Janet said, "About how you don't like kids. You never want to be tied down with a family."

"Oh my god. Janet…" Andrew took her face in his hands. "She was lying. It was all lies."

Unsure, Janet looked up at Andrew. *Could he be telling the truth?* Those blue eyes were intense as they stared back at her. She remembered how great he was with Oba…how kind he was with that little girl earlier this evening. His eyes told her what she needed to know. Fiona had been lying to her.

Then, what she had said seemed to register on his face. "Wait. You're pregnant? Right now?"

Janet smiled and nodded. "Yes! I found out a few weeks ago."

Andrew dropped back down to his knees and pressed his face up against Janet's satin dress. "Hello… hello. It's me. Your daddy. I can't wait to meet you.

Your mama and brother and I are going to give you the best life. We will be a family. Forever."

Janet could hardly believe it. She and Andrew would raise the baby and Oba... they would be a family.

And with that, Andrew stood and pulled Janet to her feet. At the top of the London Eye, with the full moon lighting the raindrops, and the lights of London illuminated like a Monet painting, Andrew slipped the diamond ring on Janet's finger, looked into her eyes and before he kissed her, said, "You are beloved."

EPILOGUE

"Mama, do I have to growl when I walk down the aisle?" Oba looked so handsome in his suit. He was fidgeting with the white flower pinned to his jacket.

"What do you mean, little king?

"If I am the ring bear, don't I need to growl?"

The women all laughed, and Janet kissed the top of her son's head affectionately. "No, my love. You just be you."

It was one year to the day after that fateful night. The documentary.. the Ferris Wheel… the night spent in her Penthouse Suite after she'd agreed to become his wife. The happy and proud day in court when Oba became their son...They all seemed like distant, yet cherished memories.

Today was the day Andrew would make good on his promise to marry her. This was their wedding day.

Oba had gone into the "Man room" to be with Andrew and his best men. When he'd told the other members of the BBC 2 that he and Janet were finally getting married, they started arguing over who should be best man.

"I was his roommate." "Yeah, but I introduced him to Janet." "Yeah, but I look better in a tux."

In the end, it was Winston who suggested, "Why is it the custom to only have one best man? Why not have all three?" And so he did.

For Janet, the choice was clear. Nicole was the only one who could be her maid of honor. Not only did they go back the farthest, but if it weren't for her, none of this would have happened.

Putting the final touches on her makeup, Janet reflected on the year. When they had gotten back to Francistown (after stopping off at the Apple Store in London to get a new phone), Janet and Andrew threw themselves into their projects.

For Andrew, the diamond mine he purchased turned out to be the most profitable one to date. And with the new sustainable mining methods, he felt comfortable that it was ethical as well as profitable.

The adjacent plots had been developed with the help of Ryan and his family's construction company. Cole infused some additional capital into the project, and now every one of Francistown's 100,000 residents had updated water, electrical, and HVAC systems.

Plus, they had conspired on one other project, dubbed The Hidden Gem. For months, the men would take day trips to who knows where and come back all dusty and sweaty.

For Janet, the infusion of cash from the gala meant that she could update and renovate A Place for Grace. Plus, they had finished construction on Extended Grace, and there were several families already living there. It was still heartbreaking to see, but at least Janet could keep them together as they faced the crisis as a family.

The additional resources, plus the donations and material support that came from the documentary, Amazing Grace, meant that Janet could expand the orphanage, and was able to make it into a self-sustaining charity. Janet no longer needed to take money from the Girard Foundation.

"You look like you're ready for a glass of champagne." Coral handed her a flute and toasted. "I am so happy for you, friend."

Looking around at the wedding preparations, Janet thought, *What an incredible day. Everything is perfect. Wait...you know what that means...*

Sure enough, there was a knock on the door. Without waiting for an answer, Alexis Girard breezed in. "Ladies. May I have the room?"

Grinning, Nicole, Elyse, Radhika, and Coral all filed out.

"Mother. I thought you were with Daddy in the waiting area."

"I was, but I wanted a moment alone with you. It's not every day that your only daughter gets married."

"True, but the ceremony is about to start."

With an expansive sweep of her hand, Alexis said, "Darling. It's not like they can start without you."

Janet laughed and took another sip of champagne. "Okay. Fine. Out with it. What are the pearls of wisdom you have for me?"

Alexis got strangely quiet. "They aren't pearls of wisdom. It's an apology. I haven't been a very good mother to you. I realized on the flight over here that I was jealous of you."

Janet sat back in shock.

"You are so beautiful and strong. You forged a life

for yourself that is full of depth and meaning. When I got pregnant with you, I did the opposite. I folded my life into your father's. I gave up my dreams to become a mother. And I resented you for it."

"Mom…"

"No, wait. I have to finish or I won't be able to get it out. My wish for you, Janet, is that you know the joy in your husband and children that I never had. Not that it wasn't there, but I didn't look for it. I was looking for a life that didn't exist, when I had everything I needed right here. With you."

Crying, the mother and daughter embraced for several minutes. "Oh, now look. We've messed up our makeup. Let's get someone in here to fix it…"

Standing outside the door that led into the chapel, Janet heard her father's voice. "Are you ready?" Squeezing his hand, she nodded. *I've never been more ready for anything in my life.*

The organ music began, and Coral walked down the aisle, holding baby Gouta. Janet was so happy that Andrew had agreed to name their daughter after Oba's birth mother. The baby's dark ringlets bounced as her godmother Coral carried her and gave her flower petals to drop. Watching the petals float to the ground was a wonderful game to Gouta, and she giggled all the way down the aisle.

Next was Oba. Six years old and standing tall, he was so serious about balancing the rings on the pillow he carried. It was an important task, they'd told him. And he took it to heart.

Their friends were next, walking down the aisle arm in arm. First, Michael and Elyse. Then, Cole and Radhika. Finally, Nicole and Ryan walked together. Ryan still had a slight limp from the accident, and Nicole's arm was steadying as he held it. Was it Janet's imagination, or was there some chemistry there?

Before she had a chance to contemplate that further, the music changed. Everyone stood to face her. The bridal march commenced, and Janet and her father slowly made their way around the aisle. Janet was blown away as she looked around. The entire church was filled to standing room capacity with members of the community. The children from A Place for Grace had formed a choir and would sing the recessional hymn. Claudia was there, next to Winston and David. Everyone that she knew and loved was in one place...

As Janet's father passed her hand from his to

Andrew's, her heart swelled. This was what life was all about. Love and family. Serving others. Making life better, every day.

Hand in hand, eye to eye, together, Janet and Andrew said, "I do."

"I am going to fall. I can't see where I'm walking!" Janet was gripping Andrew's arm. Blindfolded, he had whisked her away after the wedding reception.

"Do you want to see The Hidden Gem or not? We can turn around if you want?" Andrew was being playful.

"No, no. I have been dying to see this mysterious project of yours for months. Every time I ask anyone in town, they just look away and change the subject. It's a conspiracy!"

"Okay, then. Are you ready?"

"Am I ever!"

Andrew removed Janet's blindfold and caught her as she went weak in the knees.

"Oh my god. Andrew. Is this…?"

"Yes, Red. It's our home. The one we dreamed about that weekend in the Hamptons."

"How did you? I mean, this is Africa…" Janet was agape at the huge white house that stood before her. It was an exact replica of the house they had dreamed of building so many years ago."

"I told you. I have friends everywhere." He grinned, as he lifted her up to carry her over the threshold.

"It's so beautiful."

"No…our family is beautiful." Andrew carried his wife into their home, where Oba and Gouta waited. As they closed the door, Janet noticed a sign over the fireplace that said, "You are Beloved."

ALSO BY MOLLY SLOAN

Beholden to you

https://dl.bookfunnel.com/kq1zzfidj4

Coming Soon:
Beguiled by You

FREE GIFTS / EMAIL LIST

Free copy of Beholden to You

ABOUT THE AUTHOR

Molly Sloan is a second generation Irish American who traded her early modeling career for public relations. After 10 years developing business strategy, branding and crisis communication for some of the world's largest companies, she is living her dream of being a writer. "I love the psychological motivation behind the characters and exploring the emotional and intimate sides of relationships," says Molly, "my books are an escape, I hope readers think so too. Every book is a standalone story with a happy ever after ending." Molly lives in Oregon with her hot husband of 20 years and her little black kitty.

Follow her on Facebook at
www.facebook.com/mollysloanauthor

Made in the USA
Monee, IL
02 January 2020